THE
HEART
OF THE
LEOPARD CHILDREN

Global African Voices

DOMINIC THOMAS, EDITOR

THE

HEART

OF THE

LEOPARD CHILDREN

WILFRIED N'SONDÉ

Translated by
Karen Lindo

Foreword by Dominic Thomas

Indiana University Press
BLOOMINGTON & INDIANAPOLIS

This book is a publication of

Indiana University Press
Office of Scholarly Publishing
Herman B Wells Library 350
1320 East 10th Street
Bloomington, Indiana 47405 USA

iupress.indiana.edu

Original publication in French
© 2007 Actes Sud

Library of Congress Cataloging-in-Publication Data

Names: N'Sondé, Wilfried, author. | Lindo, Karen, translator.
Title: The heart of the leopard children / Wilfried N'Sond?e ; translated by
    Karen Lindo ; foreword by Dominic Thomas.
Other titles: Coeur des enfants léopards. English
Description: Bloomington : Indiana University Press, 2016. | Series: Global African voices
Identifiers: LCCN 2015047348 | ISBN 9780253021908 (pbk. : alk. paper)
Subjects: LCSH: Africans – France – Fiction. | Immigrants – France – Fiction. |
    Youth – France – Fiction.
Classification: LCC PQ3989.3.N76 C7413 2016 | DDC 843/.92 – dc23
LC record available at http://lccn.loc.gov/2015047348

1 2 3 4 5   21 20 19 18 17 16

I dedicate this book
to my parents
Marie-Joséphine and
Simone 'Wapiti,'
Thank you. . .

*. . . From this land of which I have been robbed,
mother what turmoil my life is!*

SERGE "MNSA" N'SONDÉ

From hazardous storms, we become more beautiful!

WILFRIED PARACLET N'SONDÉ

CONTENTS

FOREWORD

The Heart of the Leopard Children: Ancestral Memory and the Creative Imagination

*B*orn in 1968 in the Republic of the Congo (Brazzaville), Wilfried N'Sondé moved to France in 1973 and grew up there in an outlying urban area of Paris. The author of four novels published by Actes Sud, one of France's most prestigious publishers, *Le cœur des enfants léopards* (The Heart of the Leopard Children, 2007), *Le Silence des esprits* (The Silence of the Spirits, 2010), *Fleur de Béton* (Flower in Concrete, 2012), and *Berlinoise* (2014), he has received considerable critical attention and been recognized with important literary awards, most notably the Prix des Cinq Continents de la Francophonie and the Prix Senghor de la création littéraire. N'Sondé also publishes short stories and essays, his work has been adapted for the stage, and he has established a reputation in Berlin, where he moved in 1989 after the fall of the Berlin Wall and shortly before German reunification, as a pioneering musician and performer of afro-punk, rock trash, slam, and spoken-word.

N'Sondé is considered one of the shining lights of African, Afropean, and French writing. However, he is a writer who both exceeds and resists categorization, questioning the pertinence and even the validity of such mechanisms and in so doing, complicating attempts at circumscribing his work. As he contends, "The ethno-identitarian

machine has become a deadly poison. . . . It has a tendency to region-
alize and to persist in confining art and people to the arbitrariness
of geography, to use questionable criteria in order to divide and cat-
egorize, driving us gradually further away from the essence of being
and magic of words."[1] These questions are central in his first novel,
The Heart of the Leopard Children, a work that "deals with the question of origin; human beings are not sites. Those are purely mental
constructs. What am I supposed to answer when asked 'Where do
you come from?' Congo, France, Berlin, Seine-et-Marne, Brazzaville? No. I come from my mother's womb. We don't have roots, we
are not plants."[2]

   Yet, these, and related questions – postcolonial African society,
diasporic identity, race relations, immigration policy, *banlieues* housing projects, and so forth – feature prominently in his work and pro-
vide readers with demanding and thought-provoking examples of
how the literary imagination is able to appraise these and analogous
issues. N'Sondé exhibits a concerted engagement with identity and
belonging and close scrutiny of the ways in which geographic up-
rooting impacts those who have grown in French housing projects,
on the "ambivalent"[3] physical boundaries of society and emotional
margins of "Frenchness."[4] A process of introspection defines the un-
named central protagonist's quest to seek answers to life's existential
challenges. "Where do you come from?" (p. 2), are you "Black on the
outside, white on the inside!" (p. 23), and "What are you anyway,
French or African?" (p. 76). These are the questions with which he
is confronted on a quotidian basis, and as N'Sondé has claimed, "In
writing the novel I realized that the other characters, who did not
come from the Congo, were nevertheless, in their quest for life, also
leopard children, to the extent they shared in the ferocity and rage
they brought to bear on life, but also in the same nobility of heart."[5]
Writing thus provides the occasion to "insert some humanity into
everyday news stories and to give a face, a heart, and feelings to a
segment of French society, namely poor immigrants."[6]

In *The Heart of the Leopard Children*, the central protagonist delivers, from a prison cell where he is being held in conjunction with the death of a police officer, an internal monologue that reckons with his childhood, adolescence, and young adult life, in a universe composed of interactions with the two other key figures in his life, namely his girlfriend Mireille (a Jewish *pied-noir* of Algerian descent) and his best friend Drissa (like him, of African descent). Reviewing his past provides the opportunity to question the ideals and values of the French Republic, to place these concepts and principles under pressure, in other words to test other forms of cultural, political, and social confinement, "the conviction in a color-blind ideology that has for a longtime sustained segregation in housing, discrimination in hiring practices, the reiteration of protracted historical amnesia in-school curricula and quelled the brimming buried rage by executing the long arm of the law" and "the physical isolation and alienation of *banlieues* communities from active participation within the Republican institutions that oversee the daily practices of citizenry remains startling."[7]

In the following excerpt from *The Heart of the Leopard Children*, we can observe the tenuous conjunction between experience and personal development, the confrontation with racism and the awakening of consciousness:

The teacher, who really liked him, asked him to talk about his home country. He went up to the board, turned around, and faced the class. Not knowing what to say, he smiled, mumbled two, three fragments of history about ancestors, threw in a lion here, a banana tree there, and a village made from terra cotta that he'd seen on television the night before. He decided to leave the spirits out of it. It's way too easy for them to see us as primitive and stupid. When he was done, everyone was silent, wanting to hear more. Drissa, you should have had a teacher like mine. She would take my notebook and ask me to keep a few steps back from her, don't be angry my child but that odor, you understand, I'm just not used to it. She would shake her head, left to right,

her palm elegantly placed in front of her mouth and nose. Personally, I liked
her, like a child hungry for affection. She was so refined, not to mention the
lovely pink lipstick she wore with her smile. So, the good and patient boy that
I was, I would remain a good distance from her. That's good, my boy. (p. 12)

N'Sondé's recourse to social realism thus gives a voice to those
"invisibles of the French Republic,"[8] who are so often the subject of
media and official governmental focus, yet only rarely included in
the broader national conversation.[9]

In *The Heart of the Leopard Children*, N'Sondé draws inspiration
from Kongo mythology, ancestral stories, and the recurrence of the
figure of the leopard in these narratives and memories, collectively
mined here for the purposes of the novel, "a cultural imaginary
steeped in an African cosmology."[10] He writes, "Later on, we will
dive body and soul into the Bakongo country, under the protective
eye of the invisible eternal leopards, sit at the tombs of our ancestor without fear of sorcerers or witch doctors" (p. 37). Nonetheless,
as Srilati Ravi has observed, in N'Sondé's first three novels, "the
impoverished Parisian *banlieues* serve as principle backdrop to the
stories of second-generation immigrants. . . . While these narratives
offer a realistic depiction of the life of immigrants (of all ethnic and
religious affiliations) who are economically, socially and ethnically
marginalized from mainstream society, they also contain in their
unfolding the redemptory poetry of hope and shared understand-
ings."[11] The 2008 French Nobel Prize laureate J.-M. G. Le Clézio
fastens on this dimension, stating that "I am also very fond of francophone literature outside of France. Alain Mabanckou is someone quite remarkable, and so is Wilfried N'Sondé, the author of *The
Heart of the Leopard Children*."[12] When the narrator recalls an out-
ing into Paris with his beloved Mireille, the intensity of N'Sondé's
poetic sensibility and passion are palpable:

Mireille, oh Mireille, our meeting place, Place Saint-Michel, you in your
flowery dress, and beneath, your perfume in which I would drown myself.
Your warm lips with the taste of the rain, sweet venom, and a velvety kiss

teasing my own lips. The wine of lovers. With a shared will to be good to each other, Paris became our conquered kingdom and opened itself up to us. Mireille, oh Mireille, I have fallen Mireille, a falcon with broken wings, a wild cat in captivity. I'm in prison, Mireille. Defiled, I have fallen so low. My darling, my secret, Mireille, oh Mireille, what is love, Mireille? Is it my tongue on your moist flower, when you murmur, no not there. Your eyes close a little bit, your lips trembling, you take my head between your tense fingers and passionately imprison my face in your hands. Your whole body melts ever so slowly, burning under my weight. Mireille navigating back and forth, my desire capsized in your storm. You whisper to me, don't stop. I carry us into a marvelous shipwreck. Your cries and moans make a symphony. It's a lover's hymn. Without ever saying I love you, for that would be too banal for you. Mireille, those afternoons in my room on the ninth floor, on the roofs of Paris, the yellow light of the sun on your bare body, ornate with pearls of perspiration. These are the real jewels of lovers! (p. 13)

Aesthetics and politics are indistinguishable in the architecture of the world N'Sondé builds. "In the meanwhile," as Karen Lindo writes, "as part of the creative possibilities by which the French cultural imaginary may flourish, the literary landscapes of writers like Wilfried N'Sondé paint their murals, which if we look close enough do color in the hope of belonging in postcolonial France."[13]

N'Sondé's journey has, as he himself recognizes, made him into "a cultural mosaic of sorts,"[14] and it is perhaps not surprising that he was to find in the new German capital "a culture of tolerance."[15] Somewhat paradoxically,

This distance, moreover, made it easier for me to begin to understand the archaisms and contradictions that were specific to French culture. I realized that the decision to come to Germany had allowed me to finally distance myself from a kind of hexagonal schizophrenia: that of being at once a French citizen whose equal rights were clearly and loudly affirmed but yet whose skin color gave rise to such great rants and ravings that I became increasingly skeptical of what was still being taught at university. Only too accustomed to police checks and the standard disregard for formalities and the patronizing use of the familiar "tu," I quickly had to learn to answer their stupid questions and accept the humiliation if only to avoid a more serious incident. I soon came to realize that this recurrent police harassment was inversely proportionate to the whiteness of one's complexion.[16]

Notes

1. Wilfried N'Sondé, "Ethnidentité," in Michel Le Bris and Jean Rouaud, eds., Je est un autre: Pour une identité-monde (Paris: Editions Gallimard, 2010), 100.

2. Fabienne Arvers, "Entretien avec Wilfried N'Sondé, auteur du Cœur des enfants-léopards," Les Inrockuptibles, March 12, 2011, http://www.lesinrocks .com/2011/03/12/arts-scenes/scenes/entretien-avec-wilfried-nsonde-auteur -du-coeur-des-enfants-leopards-1118636/ (accessed August 19, 2015).

3. See Véronique Bragard, "Parisian Alternative Cartographies: Meandering the Ambivalent Banlieue in Wilfried N'Sondé's Fiction," in Pascale de Souza and H. Adlai Murdoch, eds., Metropolitan Mosaics and Melting-Pots: Paris and Montreal in Francophone Literatures (Newcastle upon Tyne: Cambridge Scholars Publishing, 2013), 136–155.

4. See for example Dominic Thomas, Black France: Colonialism, Immigration, and Transnationalism (Bloomington: Indiana University Press, 2007), and Charles Tshimanga, Didier Gondola, and Peter J. Bloom, eds., Frenchness and the African Diaspora: Identity and Uprising in Contemporary France (Bloomington: Indiana University Press, 2009).

5. Vitraulle Mboungou, "Wilfried N'Sondé livre 'Le cœur des enfants léopards,'" Afrik.com, May 19, 2007, http://www.afrik.com/article11755.html (accessed August 19, 2015).

6. Mboungou, "Wilfried N'Sondé livre 'Le cœur des enfants léopards.'"

7. Karen Lindo, "N'Sondé's Post-2005 Youth Mural: Exploring Afro-Europe in Wilfried N'Sondé's Literary Landscape," in Dominic Thomas, ed., Afroeuropean Cartographies (Newcastle upon Tyne: Cambridge Scholars Publishing, 2014), 113.

8. See for example Achille Mbembe, "The Republic and Its Beast: On the Riots in the French Banlieues," translated by Jean Marie Todd, in Charles Tshimanga, Didier Gondola, and Peter J. Bloom, eds., Frenchness and the African Diaspora: Identity and Uprising in Contemporary France (Bloomington: Indiana University Press, 2009), 47–69.

9. For an overview of other works in this genre, see Romuald-Blaise Fonkoua, "Ecrire la banlieue: la littérature des 'invisibles,'" in Nicolas Bancel, ed., Le retour du colonial, Cultures du Sud 165 (April–June 2007), 89–96.

10. Lindo, "N'Sondé's Post-2005 Youth Mural," 115.

11. Srilati Ravi, "Toward an Afropean Cosmopolitanism: Hospitality, Friendship and the African Immigrant," in Nicki Hitchcott and Dominic Thomas, eds., *Francophone Afropean Literatures* (Liverpool: Liverpool University Press, 2014), 138.

12. François Dufay, "J.-M. G. Le Clézio: On ne peut pas faire barrage au métissage," *L'Express*, October 10, 2008, http://www.lexpress.fr/culture/livre/jmg -le-clezio-on-ne-peut-pas-faire-barrage-au-metissage_587614.html?p=2 (accessed August 19, 2015).

13. Lindo, "N'Sondé's Post-2005 Youth Mural," 126.

14. Mboungou, "Wilfried N'Sondé livre 'Le cœur des enfants léopards.'"

15. Arvers, "Entretien avec Wilfried N'Sondé."

16. Wilfried N'Sondé, "Francastérix," translated by Karen Lindo, in Nicki Hitchcott and Dominic Thomas, eds., *Francophone Afropean Literatures* (Liverpool: Liverpool University Press, 2014), 204.

THE
HEART
OF THE
LEOPARD CHILDREN

PROLOGUE

*F*rom Vancouver to Brasilia, from the gangsters in New York, Bahia, Lagos, behind the bars at the Fleury-Mérogis prison, on the benches of the amphitheaters at the Sorbonne, for some of the junkies at the central station in Amsterdam, for the AIDS orphans of Mombasa, the commuters pressed and packed into the RER train on line A heading into Paris, for the memories of the deceased watching over *Kongo*, all the faces of voodoo ceremony participants in Haiti, those buried for centuries below the African continent, beneath the uniforms of ear-cutting Senegalese soldiers, the drug addicts, the fanatics, those stuck in the trenches in the Flanders during the Great War, the bones of those scattered at the bottom of the Atlantic, the asylum seekers, the EU authorities, for the female vendors in the Brixton market, the jubilation of the sound systems in Jamaica, and especially for those genocided in Rwanda,

. . . Africa haunts our black skin.

———

Questions, always questions, they'll never stop, will they! I have a hard time figuring out where I am. The captain keeps blaring questions at me and I can't follow what he's saying. It's late. I have had too much to drink and smoked way too much. He needs to cut it out! He probably doesn't even realize that I'm in no condition to answer him. At least open a window, please! No, he persists, telling me to shut up for Christ's sake, reminds me I'm in police custody! I'm in

1

so much pain. In all this confusion, I can see the silhouette of my ancestor, beside himself!

Son, is this why you came to France? I'm afraid of the interrogation. All the years of nonstop questions have encumbered my brain. Who are you? Where do you come from? Did you work hard in school? What's it like where you come from?

I feel like I'm caught up in a whirlwind of chaotic images. Hazy thoughts are coming at me, one after the other in full force. They're like flashes of my life. I glimpse my ancestor rising up. He stands awkwardly. He is surrounded by the glow of the benevolent spirits. Hallucinating, his gaze extends beyond the living, his words, I can still hear them very clearly . . .

You must always believe. Stay strong. Faith moves mountains. Don't be a bystander in life. No. Take it by the reins. Lay it down beneath you like a woman, a real woman with curves like a prayer pillow. Embrace it gently, at other times intensely. Seek out the source of life, where it pulsates, where it burns hot and humid, here, there, everywhere. The world is yours for the taking. Learn to feel out the world. Always give the best of yourself. Bite into it and don't hold back. Fear; leave it behind, far away from you. It will pass through you and continue its course. Walk like a God among men. Always consider what your actions say about you. Every step resonates; yours levitate! Be mindful of the way you carry yourself, especially when life punches you right in the heart, your body. Spit violently on the ground if you have to. Turn a deaf ear to the mean-spirited and narrow-minded. They can only drag you into the lair of regrets, jealousy, and resentment.

Aside from the words, there is also this presence that is difficult to describe. When the invisible ones come to me, they deliver each syllable directly into my soul, and this gesture charges them with even graver significance. It's such a powerful sensation that I can feel it under my skin, like the touch of a tender lover. My whole body is taken in by it, enlivened by these words.

Bite your lip when life gets too hard, when it gnaws away at those wounds buried deeply within you. You will never know loneliness. You are a link in the eternal chain, the hyphen without which everything else would fall apart. From time to time, allow yourself to get shaken up a bit, so that you can reconnect with your dreams, to the space of travel, to the immaterial world of those who have gone on before you. This is where you will find the keys to yesterday, today and tomorrow, discover the never-ending source of a good heart that knows how to love, console, and heal. Learn to channel this strength, this energy, because it can overwhelm you, and if you're not careful, lead to insanity. It is like a pool of black light in which images and solemn words dance wildly together.

This is what my ancestor liked to talk about, standing proud and exuberant in his dark blue suit, always barefoot, because there wasn't a pair of shoes in the world that hadn't been scared off by his deformed toes. With his words and deeds, he became, once more, fully alive. He beamed. In fact, long before me, it was probably he who had been in need of these long monologues, this food for the soul.

When you fall, get up again, wipe away your tears. You are a revolutionary. Like the earth, turn, turn, and turn again, never stop turning. Dare to enter into battle, and once you've finally overcome all the obstacles and elegantly eliminated your worst enemies, show yourself a winner. But always remain humble. Don't forget your history, where you come from, where you're going. Don't forget the bush, the jungle, the leopards, and the spirits who call and act above and beyond the chains of servitude. They are great because they have conquered death. Listen with your skin to understand these images, immerse yourself fully into them, they will guide you, like faithful, tireless geometricians.

Solemn and dignified, he picked up his shirt and discovered a light brown spot, imprinted on his skin, in the lower back. A ferocious black leopard had licked him there one day, just as he had done with his father before him. My grandfather, as the story goes, was a legendary hunter whose fury was such that he could make a wild cat urinate from fright. When his wrath thundered throughout the village, the entire region would steer clear of him, animals and White men alike.

Leopards used to rule this country, long before us. First, they chased us out mercilessly and then one day. . . . No one really knows anymore. Son, leave behind your logic with your fine suit and well-polished shoes. We haven't found a way to explain it, but one thing is certain, we were discovered, some of us were in the bush and the jungle, others perched in hundred year-old trees. We had all been nursed at the breast of protective wild cats, whose gaze was earnest and gentle, and been caressed by their deadly velvet paws. It was that period that marked the beginning of the history of our country, the Kingdom of Kongo.

Stay fresh. Stay open and awake to the balancing act, the great art, the new adventure that is life, waiting for you. The tightrope walker that you are will have no trouble balancing above continents, worlds, and times. Stand tall, proud, smile and cherish life, it is your singular treasure. Be a craftsman of change for without this we won't amount to much tomorrow. It is time to get back to who we really are, to what we have always been.

Drissa is also here, tears in his eyes, fascinated. He is drinking the words of the ancestor, as though they were finally quenching and unburdening the profound thirst of his soul. I can see on his face a mixture of fear and anxiety. Mireille is here, too. These words have lulled her childhood and perhaps even saved her, brought her closer to whom she really is.

The ancestor continues. What would your grandfather say? Courageous, steadfast in his convictions, he fled the hell of the Congo-Ocean Railway, the bloodbath, every day there were new deaths! Yes Ma'am, dynamite in the anus, at work, nothing but a bunch of lazy black asses! All this so that, one night, you would wind up in a police station, no longer able to speak, your head in your hands. Don't play innocent with me. It's far too late for that!

I have a weird kind of soup in my mouth, a bit of snot, tears. I can't seem to spit it all out. Saliva and blood, running from my lips. The captain hits really hard once he decides to go at it. There must be a mistake, captain. I didn't do anything wrong, I was just partying. Stop treating us like idiots. It was you. Everyone saw you. We have witnesses.

The captain couldn't care less. It must be part of his training. He is scarlet red. I want him to stop. I want to lie down. I had too much to drink. My whole body feels sick. I don't even have it in me to change positions. I just can't. I can't coordinate my movements. A myriad of images are all whirling around, jostling about, creating this huge block between my brain and my eyes. It's been going on for so long now, I just can't keep up. A uniformed officer is trying to calm the captain down. I've seen this in the movies, one plays bad cop, the other good cop. Captain, black cat, slayer or scavenger? She holds him back. He might have killed me. Stop, please, otherwise, I'm going to explode!

Lady officer, you have nothing better to do than torture citizens? She is surprisingly pretty, a bit uptight in her unflattering blue pants. They make her look like a shapeless square, make her ass flat. I am trying to size her up, just like the ancestor taught me to do, trying to see what's in her heart, look beyond whatever it is she is giving off. Come on, lady officer, come out from behind that cruel legal mask you're wearing. . . . You're not like the captain, rejoicing. His soul is all dried up, all done up in his horrific looking duds. I spit you out officer. Today and tomorrow are like party time for him. He gets to leave his mediocre den. On the streets you don't even exist. I walk right past you and don't even see you. He is holding me up now. He adjusts his tie. He must be all excited. The hour of the wolf has come.

You too, my captain, I manage to get a glimpse of you out there in space. You know, my friend, I do business with the occult powers. I can already imagine you as a child, timid and clumsy. You suffered because of your height, your body and that dull complexion, which has been with you your whole life. Whimpering during those lonely nights, your fingers wedged between your legs, your soiled sheets, and your tears. You were that kind of kid who enjoyed sneakily torturing harmless insects. I can just see your sick jubilation.

I am off the hook. Quick snapshot, your bitterness as you grinded on your vengeance, leaning over protecting your treaties about personal privacy. Unpopular, starved for affection, your cruelty made you ashamed of yourself. It left you isolated, left you with a strange sense of self-satisfaction. Executioner's delight. You have decided that the other is a hateful and cynical pack. You're up in the front row, but you're all alone, the most scathing of the lot. You take off every morning as far away as you can go, secure in the comfort of the cold steel of your weapon, beating against your hip, perfectly following the rhythm of your day.

To be this cruel, this guy really has to be afraid of me! He tries to speak about me or about someone who technically resembles me. He's saying a bunch of things he must have learned by heart. He goes on, spouting off his prejudices, and I don't understand a word he's saying. Leave me alone. I have a headache. Officer, you are boring me to death. You're playing a broken record. The world isn't just about your Penal Code, your Bible, the daily news at 1 o'clock and at cocktail hour, and between football and the weather report, the disturbing brouhaha about the dark-skinned, kinky-haired youth. And let's not even talk about the worst of it, young girls prostituting themselves just about everywhere, which of course we know doesn't prevent you from enjoying your Sunday roast at your mother-in-law's. Look at me, me too, I have a family. Why don't you ask me how it's going sometime with a smile? Life isn't just all about you and your church and your bells ringing in the countryside, all done up in your new outfits, looking all spiffy. I'm the one talking to him now and not so kindly either. Think about your village. I stand up. Don't detain me. Open up your eyes.

This is a one-of-a kind scene, a trembling of humanity because in the quiet of the country everyone knows everyone for generations, everyone says good morning to everyone, baguette under the arm while leaving the bakery owned by the brother-in-law, before going to see your buddies at the counter of the local bar. All of a sudden there comes this hydraulic, metallic monster with breaks, mechanical technology, computing, and all the rest of it. It all culminates in the majestic R E R that has essentially forever torn into the tranquility of these parts. This immense mountain of steel shooting into city hall, right at the foot of the blue-white-red flag and just before the monument honoring those who gave their lives for France. It is superbly decorated with obscene graffiti, indecipherable codes, filthy; it delivers its load of faces, of religions, and of colors during your precious campaigns. During business hours, the doors open to the sound of sirens, and quietly pour out their share of an eighteen-hour day. Out come the Rastas, a festival of baseball caps worn backward, all coming to a banquet of couscous and mafé stew, veiled women yelling joyfully, their piercing yoo-hoos, high-pitched guitars releasing diabolical rhythms, Kinshasa style, na lingi yo, a festival of bright-colored boubous doing the ventilator dance, mothers going about in a carefree manner, their horde of noisy, snot-nosed kids, one on each hand, one on their back, pregnant with twins and another one perched on top of their head. Adolescents, dressed in tight short outfits, moving their protruding buttocks; the way they move their curves could destroy a priest's career. Black frizzy hair, all greased up from the government family allowances. Come on captain, why don't you get a ticket and come to my country? Don't worry, I'll show you around the country of the leopard children, where the trees flirt with the sky, so tall they can almost touch it. On the way, we'll stop by my crib where we hang out and goof off in building hallways. I'll take you to a place where we live side by side with the dead. I'll teach you to speak to them, just like they do with me in my head, and you'll close your eyes and see the light, yes, the light before you, a few inches from your forehead! I'll tell you about Mireille and her all-knowing figures in my mouth.

Kamel is one of the last travelers. I've known him since our schooldays and time in the sandbox. He shows up all dignified, Koran in hand. He wants to forgive the whole world, a real patriarch under that full beard, as dated as his outfit, because just recently, he rediscovered the road to the mosque. Unsure of his footing, he advances all the same in his babouche slippers. This is a real miracle for someone who, as a child, never imagined that there was any other will in the universe but his own.

Drissa is also coming to city hall, handsome, all smiles. Now he has gone and spoilt the whole picture, showing up in his young-immigrant-inner-city-kid outfit, the social case, psychologically unstable. Drissa, I'm sighing deeply, my friend, my brother, my refuge. The kids in the neighborhood say he's crazy in the head. Ever since the sanitized "white coats" took him away in his camisole while kids were dancing around a gloomy looking cortege, twisting themselves up in a kind of strange dance. Others were clapping in tempo. Today is a big day of celebration. A mother howls her sadness, hysterical, she rips off her outfit, piece by piece, tears, her hairdo a complete mess. Drissa, Drissa! Almost naked, she kneels down, raises her hands to the sky, they fall, she begins again, two times, ten times or more, again and again. In the end, there is only pain and silence. Police officers form a circle securely around his marabout uncle, a powerless witness to the scene. Drissa? Drissa, what happened to you?

Take all of that, all the same, Mister captain. It frightens your catechism to hear all of this, right? You're going on like you don't understand, index on your temple. Take off your uniform, your helmet; let's go party with the devils and Mami Wata, the female spirit of the waters! Shift into a higher gear and let's head to some of the world's more vertiginous heights. Take your courage by the hand and let's go, at least for a short while, get away from all your certainties!

I'm yelling and struggling. There must be at least five of them holding my mouth to the ground, filled with cigarette butts, "this guy is completely crazy"; let me talk and scream, I finally have the words for what I want to say. Please, I don't want to hurt anyone. Totally panicked, take this idiot to his cell!

It's filthy and it stinks. They left me alone, hands handcuffed behind my back, my nose kissing the floor. I can't help but think of Drissa. I remember when he would come to the house to listen to my father's stories. He was afraid but he still kept coming back, especially to hear the ones about the spirits who dance naked on the walls at night. If you're quiet, and watch out for them, you can feel them brush by you, especially your forearms, they are gentle and kind. They're the ones who accompany us from birth right to the end, when we finally join them. Tell me you haven't forgotten Drissa; you can't do that! You always told Mireille and me that we were similar, like a fleet of fighter jets, we glide, we fly, we forge full speed ahead, falcons, ready to accomplish our mission. You can't grovel around looking so miserable. For our brothers and sisters, the spirit of our ancestors and all those who are back in the home country, lift your head up! Stop all your crying in my arms. Don't fade on me!

When was it, yesterday, last year? I met you at the train station. Once we got into the elevator of the Eiffel Tower, you started shaking and crying. I'm here with you, don't look down, stop shouting, calm down, everybody can hear you. Pardon him Madam, he's not doing it on purpose, I know him, it's Drissa. His uncle is a marabout, a very mild-tempered man; he gives treatments and tries to help others out as much as he can. They're from my neighborhood. His father's a city employee, works in the street-cleaning services. He works all summer long and all winter long to the point of ruining his body. When he gets home, he has to really rest his body, you understand, because of all the pain he has. His wife makes a point of chasing away any and everyone who dares to bother him. He alone provides for the whole family back in the home country. That's true, he probably shouldn't have had his second wife come to France; it created a real fucking mess. He rarely speaks to Drissa or his other kids. Ladies and gentleman, don't worry, he's not violent. His only problem is that there are too many questions; it's kind of like a thick vase in his head. Trust me, it's going to pass before you know it, thank you.

Police vehicle number 357 stopped right next to us. Standing, I held Drissa curled up, broken down in deep, loud sobbing; concerned, curious bystanders, keep their distance from us. The door opened. Of course, I was expecting the worst, operation beat down, load him up, *manu militari*, and Drissa orbiting far away on another planet, hanging on to me, a castaway getting onto a makeshift rescue raft. Criminal investigation unit, we've been called because of trouble on the main highway. I could see in his eyes that this civil servant hesitated to trust me. His hand stayed close to his club. I explain to him that it's Drissa, not a junkie; he's under medical supervision for a neurological disorder. I wanted to take him out a little and before you knew it everything went haywire. The next few seconds were as heavy as lead. Drissa doesn't have it in him to be violent; he gave up on normality ages ago. He says nothing, that way things won't escalate or go the wrong way. The agent speaks to him kindly, hand on his shoulder, asks for our address, no he's not really my brother; I politely decline his offer to drive us home. I can already see Drissa hysterical in the back of the police station wagon. Understanding and reassuring, the peacekeeper Pascal Froment, advises us to head on home quickly and not hang around here, his paternal hand at the nape of my neck, get going, now take good care of your friend! Buddy, we have seen a lot of guys like you, go on now, pull yourself together, you'll make it.

Now I'm the one in a cell. Forty-eight hours in police custody. They took away my belt, my laces and my shoes. Every time I get up I have to hold up my pants to keep them from falling down. They have left me to the stench of my own vomit. I can barely make myself out from all of this shit sticking to my clothes. Bunch of helpless sadists, torturers, racists. To avoid getting shut up or slapped around, every fifteen minutes or so, I'm spewing out my rage, my fear, my sadness to this bizarre looking lock. I have nothing in here, not a chair, not a table, just massive confusion in my head. I'm trying to remember what could have happened but am just feeling this unnerving emptiness. Hanging on to images of the past is the only thing I have to escape this place.

—∽—

When we were kids, Drissa and I used to go to the local bakery. The lady at the bakery was always smiling, they're so adorable with their little ringlets, a little touch on the cheek, and their little nappy heads, giving us candy, thanks Baker Lady. I was so amazed at the size of her breasts beneath her white coat. Baker Lady, I will always love you. It was only much later, somewhere between the ages of thirteen and fourteen that we became foreigners, delinquents, illegal workers, and started overhearing words like "integration," "immigration," barely tolerated in political agendas.

We became the face for all the misery in the world for which no one wants to pay. That same Baker Lady now follows us around with a suspicious look. She must know the captain. They probably went to the same school, the one where they teach you to make sure the doors are always locked.

She scrutinizes us, and on first glance decides we're trouble, a danger. Why do you keep coming in here? What do you want? If the lady at the bakery hadn't changed over the years, Drissa wouldn't have eventually lost it. He would have kept on smiling. But these days he's got this intense gaze fixating on some random object. Any opportunity he has, no matter where he is, he lies down and takes refuge by falling asleep.

When he does finally say something, he sounds crazy. It's like he sees too many questions coming at him, not to mention the ones that get inside your head and can't ever leave, waiting eternally for a simple, clear, sincere answer, one that reassures the person asking, oh, okay, I get it. Nope. These questions are so thick-skinned, going in circles, unrelenting, and each time posed louder and louder. When you see Drissa rolling his eyes, glazed over from all the medication, you know he's tracking them around and around. Drissa and I, we used to be friends. We could always count on each other,

I'm your screen, you're my shield, I'll dry your tears. We had totally given up on the crazy idea of trying to understand, we were simply forging ahead together, not worrying about whether we were right or wrong, just making sure we both had what we needed to survive.

At school, he was a happy kid. At that time, you could tell he didn't understand any of the questions. They would head his way and continue their course quietly without an answer from him. Surprised, the teacher would get angry. He would purse his lips a bit and then wait patiently for the next question. He never should have tried to understand them, never.

I think that's what got to him. Because one day they finally made their way in, somewhere under his skin, lodged right into his heart, stuck there, and short-circuited everything! Where do you come from? Do you know your culture? What do you do for a living? Do you have any money? Why is your uncle so weird? What's all this stupid stuff about spirits? Train ticket? Residence permit? ID? Who are you?

The teacher, who really liked him, asked him to talk about his home country. He went up to the board, turned around, and faced the class. Not knowing what to say, he smiled, mumbled two, three fragments of history about ancestors, threw in a lion here, a banana tree there, and a village made from terra cotta that he'd seen on television the night before. He decided to leave the spirits out of it. It's way too easy for them to see us as primitive and stupid. When he was done, everyone was silent, wanting to hear more. Drissa, you should have had a teacher like mine. She would take my notebook and ask me to keep a few steps back from her, don't be angry my child but that odor, you understand, I'm just not used to it. She would shake her head, left to right, her palm elegantly placed in front of her mouth and nose. Personally, I liked her, like a child hungry for affection. She was so refined, not to mention the lovely pink lipstick she wore with her smile. So, the good and patient boy that I was, I would remain a good distance from her. That's good, my boy.

It's funny. Yesterday the distance between her and me was just a few steps, today, there are bars between the captain and the quarters of my own misfortune, between their uniforms and my distress. Now there's a phrasing Mireille would have liked. . .

—ᴡ—

Mireille, oh Mireille, our meeting place, Place Saint-Michel, you in your flowery dress, and beneath, your perfume in which I would drown myself. Your warm lips with the taste of the rain, sweet venom, and a velvety kiss teasing my own lips. The wine of lovers. With a shared will to be good to each other, Paris became our conquered kingdom and opened itself up to us. Mireille, oh Mireille, I have fallen, Mireille, a falcon with broken wings, a wild cat in captivity. I'm in prison, Mireille. Defiled, I have fallen so low. My darling, my secret, Mireille, oh Mireille, what is love, Mireille? Is it my tongue on your moist flower, when you murmur, no not there. Your eyes close a little bit, your lips trembling, you take my head between your tense fingers and passionately imprison my face in your hands. Your whole body melts ever so slowly, burning under my weight. Mireille navigating back and forth, my desire capsized in your storm. You whisper to me, don't stop. I carry us into a marvelous shipwreck. Your cries and moans make a symphony. It's a lover's hymn. Without ever saying I love you, for that would be too banal for you. Mireille, those afternoons in my room on the ninth floor, on the roofs of Paris, the yellow light of the sun on your bare body, ornate with pearls of perspiration. These are the real jewels of lovers!

Me, I began to truly worship your skin, so pale, almost transparent in my eyes, especially your breasts, above the blue lines. I followed ever so gently their line with the point of my tongue. It was her favorite pastime, a cocktail of laughter in a perfume of pleasure. She always shook her head, with a tender smile, when I told her for the thousandth time, about how disgusted I used to be as a kid at the sight of veins on the skin of certain White people.

My Saturday queen, you wanted to see my eyes precisely in the moment when everything lit up and I poured myself inside you. You watched me, and you groaned deeply. In your eyes, it was November, green, brown, gray, shaking beneath your fingers, strengthening the buds at the peak of your breasts. My lips quivered, the all-white crescent moons under my eyelids, these were your trophies. You would blush as you said so. Avoiding eye contact, you buried yourself in my armpit, overindulging, close to the intoxicating perfume, the drug of lovers!

Mireille, Mireille, Mireille, my treasure, it was toward the ardent inferno, under the thick black shadow below your belly that we headed, holding onto each other, one on top of the other, right to the tip of our bodies. Together we explored our taboos. Let's rest for a while and make love again. I messed up, Mireille, and now my darling, I'm lost.

I can hear them in the corridor. All suited up in uniforms, arriving in great stride with more questions, violation to law and order, crime, assault. This is undoubtedly a nightmare. Where's the telephone so I can call my mother right away? I can already feel her sadness burning in my chest.

A little bit more about you, Mireille, about you and our story. That's the only thing that can save me now, as it has always done in the past. I can see you lying on the mattress, sun bathing your beautiful white behind, and your round, wide, curvaceous figure. I find peace in the treasure of your fluids. They shine and enchant me, have become the infinite space of my well-being. You came into my life and lay down almost from the start. I became your falcon that comes, goes, and returns again to his nest, this intimate wound where I finally found peace in the depths of your belly. They are back, Mireille. Give me some more of you, from the days of our first lovemaking when we were so young, timid, and awkward. We would steal kisses. There was no place where we could love each other. It rained so much that year. The cinema was too expensive, the park, too damp. In the basement, you said no, and you cried for a long time. I beg you to forgive me, Mireille. It's because of the neighborhood.

The guys aren't so clever, but we're really not mean-spirited either. I should have listened to you instead of pretending to be someone else. I should have been more patient.

What we had was so beautiful. Now that everything has vanished and fallen apart I can see it clearly. My timid love knew how to put aside all decency, her warm breath on my chest. Your skin is so beautiful, you must feel so good! She offered me her lips, her little round breasts, their brown flowers alert to caress my body. This fusional desire gently covered my skin, my hair. Fascinated, wild with desire, I watched her completely abandon herself. One day I will take her skin captive; I pray to drive her right to the edge. Her all-knowing tongue, hold me tight between your lips. . . . Black love, tense, burning, this smirk on your face announces the rising tide that drowns the pain. Ecstasy, an amazing feeling, when pleasure takes over and sweeps away all the taboos, and all that remains is the good stuff. She also insisted that I take her on her parent's cold, sad dining table, and she let herself go with that animal cry, amid the lingering presence of her stern father and mother. Mireille celebrated the ritual that shattered all taboos. When we were together, she let herself go, consumed by the desires of our bodies, our childhood dream became an unforgettable refrain. Don't hold back, I can take it, so much more, Mireille begged. I want to feel your teeth piercing my neck. To mark the end of some especially beautiful moments of our lovemaking, she would kneel before me and kiss my feet, humming *Carmen*!

Oh yes, dear captain, I too have lived. You can hit me as hard as you like but this you can never lock away. Put the key back in your pocket.

I have loved, I have laughed, I have cried. Listen to me as well, ancestor, I haven't always failed because love that is given just like that which is taken, the charm of it, the vertiginous effect of it, this sensation of a light cataclysm that transports you to the best and worst parts of yourself is the greatest expression of magic. Drifting along with Mireille during our love story, I saw them everywhere, mischievous spirits, as old as the times, mystical companions of orgasms, they danced, they giggled all about us. They were curious, gave us strength and an even greater desire to explore our love.

But now it's dark, Mireille, I'm scared in prison. Apparently in prison they sodomize the guys!

—⁓—

Follow us without making a scene. For now, you keep the handcuffs on. I can already see the face of the scavenger captain, his need to know everything about me, what happened, admit to whatever he needs to reassure himself, good job officer, very good for your ulcer. Just the idea of it exhausts me, not even a window where I can get some air and see the light of day. What time is it? Why do they all want me to give them sound answers? Do you come from Africa? Have you thought about your future?

There is no more reason to be afraid of me. I'm in handcuffs now, confined by four officers, left to battle with my own fucked-up self. I'm moving like a zombie, a date with the prick 24/7, day and night. Officers, why do I bother you so much? Identity papers? You would think that I actually frighten you. Residence permit? Oh, you're French? Racial profiling. Empty your pockets. Do you have a knife on you? How do you defend yourself?

Hey Warden man. I also want to have some peace, alleys of flowers, smiles, good morning miss, how are you doing missus. I don't want to see anymore spit in the stairways, argue with the drunk guy across from me, find syringes in the sandbox, Saturday nights that wind up as local news stories. Close up those bars and tobacco shops so our fathers can actually sit down and enjoy their dinner. I'd also like to have some blue in my life, walks in the parks, a beautiful car in the garage, a fresh-cut green lawn, a garden for the summer. It's a shame that you can't hear me captain, I actually had a beautiful confession for you!

The door closed, another room in the back, white overcoats seated scientifically across from me. I hear the first pile of questions. These trackers of deviances and other forms of madness can't wait to hear what I have to say. I'm going to focus intensely on Drissa; he's already been through this. Brother, you're going to help me get me through this. The one in the middle is wearing a red beard. I have to really pay attention. His presence seems to calm things down some. I'm almost relaxed although certainly on guard. If only I had it altogether. His words are audible and gentle. It's a real break from the captain's barks. He's right to warn me. Hold on to whatever you want to use against me. In any event, I have no plans to tell you anything. This one must like to make love to his wife with his perfectly groomed hands. He should have met me during the good old days with Mireille. He would have considered us a very cute couple, tasting wine on the Rue Saint-André-des-Arts, an Argentine guitarist playing flamenco music, all smiles and in love, or when we used to roll around on the lawn on the Champ-de-Mars, lost in our endless laughter. If he had known us during that time, our tenderness might have melted his heart, just watching us, heading off to Paris to study, hand in hand down the Rue de Rennes, the impression we gave of finally living, the world at our feet, welcoming us. A couple, that's it, the city and its nights just for us. It's the most beautiful thing in the world.

Today, I'm having a hard time seeing my hands, bound by those who are themselves dispossessed. At the same time, I don't want him to take me to his country for crazy people. We're going to be playing hide and seek, the first one to crack has to go. That's why I'm not going to talk to you. Call the marabout instead, it's Drissa's uncle. He will burn a few things, draw some figures in the sky, and when he moves his buffalo tail, he will insult the evil spirits, and with one great breath my grandfather will personally put everything back in order in my head and in my life. Professor, psychiatrist, or specialist of God knows what, sitting comfortably on your books, can you hear the voices in my head?

I don't really remember what happened. Somehow time just went on without me. I'm tired. It's hard to have lived for so long in a storm.

What do you think, professor? Are you hesitating? Do you think I'm weird, sadistic or just a plain old pervert? My life, I already drag it alongside me with great difficulty. Leave it to me; together we are doing the best we can. You would like to hate me but you can't help but find me somehow likeable. We share a look of complicity. There is someplace where we understand each other but we are flying side by side without ever having a real meeting of the minds. He stops for a moment before the gunk that is brewing deeply inside of me. Anger, the hotbed of pure energy, dangerous, ready to spill out everywhere and at any given time, it only requires a spark.

Try at least once to communicate with the spirits the ancestor invokes. They will tell you about the leopards and me, they will teach you about our life. Doctor man, there is no one person more important than another in my life. Only the absolute power of a good heart deserves admiration. You are looking on at me as though I were unstable, ask some of your battery of questions instead, shake up some of your certainties. This should be pretty easy for you to do since I'm already among the condemned! Don't bother wasting your time trying to compare our systems. Leave the dance of tolerance to the streets, for the times of protests for progress. To show that you actually care for me, I wouldn't be surprised to see you wearing an African tunic, or beating on a djembe drum in an ethnic dance class. But as soon as it has to do with death, you rely systematically on your pragmatism and science to analyze me! The trance, when it's not attributed to alcohol, is interpreted as hysteria and referred immediately to Saint-Anne.[1]

Go on, keep talking and run your tests all on your own, I took off a long time ago. Leave my neurons in disorder. Forget about trying to treat the ills of the leopard. This is my unique garden, the only riches I possess. Don't be so fast with your confidence, don't use my case to immediately justify and forgive everything. I was marked a

---

1. A reputed Parisian hospital in the Fourteenth Arrondissement, specializing in psychiatry and neurology, and symbolic of a mental institution.

long time ago by the authorities. I've been screaming at the top of my lungs to plead my case before the court. They have given a color to my skin and denied my existence. I have given in to the weight of the mask that tries to disfigure me. I wouldn't celebrate too soon if I were you; you can't get rid of me that easily!

When you think of me there, doctor in your white coat, know that I have the same desires as the great wild animals sequestered in cages. Ten thousand times a day, sometimes even more, they are searching for a way out, and looking at every possible angle to do so. They'll never stop. Showing their fangs, they will never give up. Go ahead, use my silence against me. Today I'm free and all you're left with is me, and now all your threats are just annoying me. Forget about me for a little while. Try to get out, at least once, from under the weight of protocol. Let me tell you about this desire I have to spit in your face, just like that, just to see your face defiled. Why don't you go and lock up, say, those who no longer make love to their wives, you would be sparing us tons of bitterness every day. Stop analyzing me and take care of the mean-spiritedness and cynicism of this world. Let me enjoy a peaceful exile. I need some quiet after all the madness, a kind of gentle respite that proud, rebellious dogs enjoy, once they are finally running in a wild nomadic pack, after having bitten their master!

Yes sir, I'm a good student, everything is going well at the university. I passed my exams. I couldn't find a decent job. I don't have the right kind of face for the ticket window! My love for Mireille, like my love for my mother, I'll keep that safe deep inside of me. You see, I'm doing the best I can. It's not easy but I'm managing, a beer, a glass of wine, a bit of weed or hashish, it's more for fun at the end of a long week. Leave me out of your statistics. Try to come and meet me where I really am or if you like I can come to you! Go on, let the sorcerers and magicians dance, they only come out to dance at night once the church and the library are closed. Get a good night's rest. Lay your head on your pillow and let them sing you to sleep. Their steps are so quiet, only the sound of their voice will resonate in your head.

Drissa knows the white overcoats only too well. From now on, they accompany him in every step of his life. The nurses take him away in the middle of the day. He was frightening everyone! Unbalanced, going berserk, wallowing in his urine, screaming his insanity. The police were already there to put his uncle in his place.

Do you know Drissa? That's my question for you. One sentence, only four words as you get up to leave the room and I block your passage. I want to go back to the cell, be among the cigarette butts, the filth, my thoughts, my leopard ancestor, with my barefoot grandfather, Drissa exhausted, drained of his whole being like a wet bird. Mireille and her cotton underpants, like when we were kids.

Push me violently against the wall of my cell, my ancestor is waiting for me!

—∞—

Ancestor, look at me, this thing in chains, a disturbing cascade, this incomplete knot, in blood and tears. This is your son, ancestor! You are looking on at me from a distance; I'm in suspension, chained down in these new lodgings. Disguised as a proud patriarch, you seem legitimate, reigning over a bunch of crazy detainees. But I'm sad for you, you also believed. What kind of legacy have you have passed on to us, what wasted freedom, laws executed by those with the most powerful arms? Promises of independence, pride reclaimed, all of it exploited, winding up with the most absurd expression of racism. Greed inaugurated the order of the day, paving the way for genocides and killings. Ancestor, you are pretending to have forgotten. As in your childhood, you are meditating, making appeals and taking refuge among the eternal invisible ones, meanwhile a cannonade continues to dominate mutilated bodies.

Charlemagne Ngouvou, Joan of Arc Maboundi, Wilfried N'Sondé, Anatole Nganga, and so many other names, what have we become, ancestor, we don't even realize that we have been handing out ridiculous sobriquets that imitate our former master? Blanche Senga, Euloge Sita, Jean de Dieu Mienandi, Anicet Boungoudiabampoutou.

. . . We have emulated the pride of the clever monkey, who can find the most unusual first name from the Catholic calendar. Ancestor, who are we really? Look at what I have become!

I have let you down, ancestor? I did my best. What can you do with me? There is no garbage can for humans! I'm bringing a little bit of you to suffer with me in my hole. Stop pretending you can't hear me with your disdainful scowl. Get down from your contempt and submit to my turmoil! I have the clarity for those who are lost. Remember how Drissa wanted to know what a Bakongo chief was, a Zulu, Kikuyu, Shona, Bamileke, Mandingo, Ashanti, Wolof. . . . His father had bought a driver's license to show off with a car that was way more than he could afford with his salary. That car meant no electricity at home, and there you were going on about great men of remarkable dignity and rectitude, who nobly executed the justice of proud and merciful men.

Ancestor, you stayed quiet, while your friend, Drissa's uncle, great marabout that he was, went on to fill his pockets by exploiting other people. Magic, the foundation that connects us all to the single broken line in life, the horizontal line that banishes right before our eyes the differences between yesterday and today. He made a business of other people's naivety and you looked the other way. He sold his powers and became a merchant of dreams and threats, all so that he could buy himself women and cars.

Where were your words in the face of this tragedy? And what of the future you silence, leaving me here to face myself? Shaking your head you say you can't understand, you grew up so far away from all of this. A couple of years in Europe and you accuse me of having forgotten who I am! Was there so little to preserve and transmit in the end?

It's high time to open a high-security national park so that I can be kept in my original ecosystem against all outside influences. Captain, professor, ancestor, grant me at least the dignity of whales, the right to exist that giant tortoises enjoy.

You can go now, ancestor. I'm not angry. I have the devil and the benevolence of the spirits. I only need the strength to rediscover love and the will to live for tomorrow.

—∾—

Who's this guy? I've been standing for hours in front of this cell. He won't stop screaming. The guy's completely nuts! A real motherfucker. A real wild animal. He gets fucked up and kills a guy by kicking him to death. No surprise they kill each other in their country, real barbarians. Why can't they just stay in their own country instead of coming here to ruin our lives? I'm getting tired of taking him back and forth for interrogation. I had to examine the inside of his mouth and his asshole. Disgusting! He fought like a wild cat. My colleagues didn't miss a beat with this piece of shit. You'd think he'd been run over by a car. Thank God my shift ends in an hour. I almost feel like letting the idiot go just so I don't have to hear him singing in African. Every time I bang on the bars for him to shut up, the more the jerk rattles on in his savage language. The guy scares me. At one point, I thought he was really some kind of sorcerer or you know some version of their weird kind of superstitions, you know like voodoo or black magic. On one of my rounds I couldn't see him anymore. The bastard had hidden under his bed. By the time I realized it, I must have lost a pound from all the worrying. I already imagined myself writing up a report explaining that the prisoner had managed to escape from the cell using supernatural powers. I was scared shitless. Naturally I had to beat up a prisoner who couldn't defend himself. It's just that he pushed me to my limits, refused to stay put. Any longer and I would have had the Disciplinary Board up my ass. Thank God this one was already so messed up that another beating didn't make any real visible difference. Right now it's feeling like things could get out of hand pretty fast. I'm dying to get out of here. At least the head honchos don't want to talk about what happened. The whole precinct feels like its spoiling for a fight. And this nut job just won't stop. He's loud, he cries, and he stinks. He does seem pretty young though for a homeless guy. Really more lost than dangerous. He's not even that big or strong. Seems to be battling his own demons. When I look in on him, it's like he doesn't even see me. I even got that feeling when I was beating him. Maybe it's the drugs. He's just as backward as the rest of them. Let's face it, it's not like these guys invented gunpowder or made an effort to do something other than music and sport. You might even think he was clever if he started running around in his tiny cell or doing some break-dancing!

When I have children, I'm going to think long and hard about where to raise them, stay clear of neighborhoods with guys like this in them. What, now I'm a racist? If everybody would just stay where they come from, we'd have way less problems. I remember the neighborhood they stole my car in. I was a student officer back then. The whole scene that night was like a riot and the investigators still haven't figured out the real reasons for all that havoc. Those assholes totally dented up my car. Pretty twisted, there was even blood on the back seat, some girl's underwear and socks. Real savages!

I'm getting off work early today. The junior officers look like they're sticking together. Given the mug they're wearing, this detainee is going to have a hell of a fifteen minutes.

—⁓—

The silence is back and it's making me think of Drissa. Drissa, what's left of you is a waste. What's a Negro, a real one? And you were already shaking! What, you weren't born over there? You don't know anything about it? You don't speak your own language? Black on the outside, white on the inside! You better hang on so you can at least make sense in these lines, otherwise you're going to wind up as a question mark. You better watch out, my friend, they want to erase you from the text. Root yourself down, anchor yourself fast, anywhere, wherever you feel good about yourself, a little parentheses that you can open, enough to slip into and have a bit of happiness before the final sentence is written.

Of Drissa, nothing is left except for a kind of black spot, indelibly stuck to his body, bye-bye, who is that one, there? You're a shameful site. Come back in another life. Who is really black? What's a White person like? His head bobs back and forth, day and night, bouncing, going from one rejection to another. You don't look like much of anything. The machine that made you went haywire. You didn't even fall from a banana tree. At least get moving behind a tam-tam! You were not written into this program. Go find a hole where you can be forgotten and let's not hear another word from you! Wear a pendant of a miniscule map of Africa in fake leather. What's a real Black person like? In any case, he doesn't look much like one! Go and bleach your skin and show your face to the world, from Johannesburg to Paris, by way of Kinshasa. Make yourself handsome! Go on, get rid of some of that color, but not too much or you'll look whitewashed, affecting a Parisian accent, and no one likes that either. Speak French eloquently and amaze the imbecile, marveled by modernity, ignorant of civilization, barefoot, bare breasts hanging all the way down to the navel in open air, with two children hanging on. Forget your CFA ways, chewed tobacco stuck to the bottom of your feet, asking once again what is the color of the White man's feces. Don't eat like a Pygmy, but don't be too delicate either, or they'll think you're acting like a White man. Who do you think you are? Don't forget your own people, the violence, the slavery, the colonies, the humiliation, the harassments, the whip. No ma'am, yes boss. Get those words out of your mouth and go enroll at the Sorbonne!

Drissa is struggling just to stand up straight. He's completely broken, beginning to think outside of his own head. The question marks are culminating inside him like lightning bolts, going from bottom to top, from yesterday to tomorrow. Today has been set aside, left in suspense, an inferno. His head and his life are too heavy for his shoulders to carry. You're not real, a mere shadow, a byline messing up the statistics just so you can sneak your way on to the metro. Sorry, but you weren't called for the casting. With a face like that, there's no role for you. Train stations, the RER, you create problems for the national education system, just more delinquency and rising high school dropout rates. He wants to stand firm, but his legs can't hold up anymore. Drissa, relax.

Listen to what the words are really saying my brother, there are men and then there's the color. Normality is in place and the minority is debated based on definitions of difference. Stop running in place. A good distance from you a satellite is talking about you. You better come to terms with the fact that there's no color in what you're doing. Did Mozart compose white music? You keep going on about how passionate you are about Negro art and black music. You better wake up, brother. You better get up to speed.

Drissa, don't let go of my hand. Think about Mireille and me. She doesn't give a shit. She only wants me. She couldn't care less about this black and white bullshit, Catholics, Muslims, Jews, Protestants, Animists. . . . For her, all these stories about spirits are nothing but pure primitive superstition!

Mireille isn't kissing the color black when she coyly tells me she wants me, her mouth on my neck and her hand running over my body. It's true that she puts on a good show when she stops by the house. She's just a schoolmate! The ancestor who has no idea who she is sends her stories and tales. She listens, smiles, and looks on at me. Her favorite tale is the one about the mistreated child, mutilated and assassinated by his mother who hated him for his beauty and who, thanks to the benevolence of the spirits, was eventually resuscitated.

Mireille sits at the table and eats with my mother. They don't speak too much with words but rather with their eyes. My mother dives into her meal with her fingers, smiling occasionally. She could never really hate White people. Mireille is especially uncomfortable when my sister asks her why she's so white. She looks on at me, her eyes beaming. The ancestor stares at her later on as if she's someone completely unfamiliar. Maybe he will always be a distracted child, always on the lookout for those unseen forces that can hinder our advancement. In any event, he instructs me to take her back home, to be a gentleman. He says it like an insult, or an order because he was never a great source of tenderness.

Drissa has forgotten our dreams, and we were such good friends. She, he and I, neighbors right from the beginning, we met each other on the gray swings next to the sandbox. Later on, Mireille would cheer us on during soccer matches in the parking lot. Drissa lived on the same floor, and Mireille lived on the third floor in the building just in front of ours. Her window was just behind the willow tree that has since been cut down. We were basically together all the time.

Very early on there was already this physical attraction between Mireille and I, but we were a one of a kind team, a fleet of falcons manipulated spiritually by the ancestors and the spirits, energized by the finesse and great ideas that Mireille had and protected by Drissa's marabout uncle. As kids, we played our games with this vague notion that we were, each one in a unique way, following our own destiny, but together. We were in our own world, away from all the other boys and their fights and the girls with their predictable love dramas. We would lay on the grass, looking up at the sky as though it were the only theater worthy of our ambitions. We would fix our gaze intensely on the stars we imagined far beyond the gray skies.

We treasured our childhood. We had no money, so we spent all our holidays with the other youth and among the five buildings in the neighborhood, along the stretch of highway that ran past our project. Our empire was in the basement. Spanish, Portuguese, Algerians, Vietnamese, Congolese, Malians, Bretons, the whole world was in the parking lot and the swimming pool which we would enter through a gap in the fencing.

Mireille, Drissa, and I, we were a one-of-a-kind team. While the boys distracted the shopkeepers, she would innocently, behind those brown curly locks and her little red freckles, steal sweets. Her angelic face dispelled any suspicion of her character. Then we would take off and share the loot in uncontrollable laughter and self-satisfaction. I can still hear it today resonating in my ears. Our behavior commanded the respect and friendship of the other children in the neighborhood. We were no longer in the category of overprotected bourgeois brats, daddy's boys. We were considered brave and earned the right to a peaceful existence. No one would dare to give us detention at the end of the school day.

We even earned the admiration of Kamel, otherwise known as Dinosaur, whose criminal reputation basically preceded his birth. Long before becoming a real criminal, dealer of hard and mild stuff, charged with assault and battery, he used to grab handbags and rob people in the streets. During almost his entire childhood and adolescence, he would break into the home of our high schoolmate Ludovic's parents' place. He started by taking their deserts while they would be having lunch outside during the summers and then went on to break into the garage and steal a bicycle. At seventeen years old, he emptied their entire home of the silver and hi-fi equipment. Ludovic was so frightened of Kamel he never dared express his suspicions. Relieved of their meager riches, the family finally decided to install the best and most expensive security system.

Later on, once Kamel had found a new way of life, thanks to his conversion to the grace of the Muslim faith, he absolutely wanted to personally apologize for all the awful things he had put them through. That's how Ludovic's mother came to find three fully bearded men ringing at her doorstep one afternoon. Within a matter of seconds, she turned as pale as a dead person, and her knees started trembling so intensely that she was about to faint. The poor woman had seen way too many television programs about Muslims, how particularly cruel the men were and how they hated women more than their worst enemies. They prayed all day long and washed their feet five times per day. She had also learned that these guys, who distributed bombs all over the place because there were so many good Christians that needed to be sent to heaven, would cut off the heads of Western tourists just for the fun of it. In the state she was in, she couldn't even hear what the youngest of the three was saying to her in the gentlest tone. As far as she was concerned, a whole scam was already in place. Like her husband had explained, this was part of a bigger scheme to basically divert her attention. These guys couldn't wait to get on to their next petty theft. One minute they were taking gunshots up the ass, the next they were fucking around with an alarm system that directly alerted the cops at the police station.

It was a game for Mireille, Drissa, and I to steal in the supermarkets, a way for us to experience fear. Given the means we had, it was just another way to use our overactive imagination. Our real country was the eternal love we had for our mothers, fixtures behind the hearth-burning fires. They were experts at negotiating in the markets. Those who had mastered French helped those who needed help. In time, they had basically reinvented the French language. I would spy on them from a distance, sitting on their bright colored mats, right by the sign that read: "Walking on the grass is prohibited." Aside from the everyday challenges they faced, they openly confided to each other about their husbands, the father of their children, the men with whom they shared an apartment. They all came from countries where a marriage based on love was an unnecessary and dangerous luxury. In the bedroom, it was next to impossible to make the difference between tenderness and procreation. Romantic love was a puerile and embarrassing idea. We grew up far away from kind words and tender hugs. We were used to major confrontations and even sometimes to physical violence, to the coldness of the cement floor and ice-cold looks.

Sadly, we often overheard these domestic fights, the screams of desperate wives, the insults of frustrated husbands, and the deafening blows. In the days that followed, the wife wouldn't show herself in public. Broken ribs hurt but heal, marks on the face fade overtime.

They talked, complained and laughed a lot, in a kind of melody that married Andalusian with Wolof, Arabic with Kikongo, intonations from the Far East blending with the seasonal sounds of the neighborhood. Even today, they have their own version of French. Integration, beware! They had been married long before they were eighteen years old and had already had several children. Not one of them really knew how to read but surprisingly they all learned pretty quickly how to count.

It's for you, and really only for you, that I am truly sorry, mother. For all those mothers who have been forgotten by history and in the news reports on the radio and television. I'm afraid to see the tears from your suffering. It's really because of you, mother, that I'm so deeply ashamed of my chains. For you and all those women, so patient and loving and who are of so little interest to anyone. In the news, only their tears make the headline, after the fact.

Mireille's parents, who are *pieds-noirs*, would have gladly eaten Arab cuisine from the neighborhood and anywhere else as a matter of fact, even three times a day, no problem. And yet they were so discreet and courteous, and worked a lot to make sure that their only child had a bright future that the Algerian War had robbed them of at her birth. They barely spoke of their past to Mireille; the topic was off limits. Her father's parents owned a café in a big city, a bomb had exploded and the younger sister, still a baby at the time had had both arms ripped apart, her face burnt, atrocious suffering, unbearable agony that had lasted for weeks. Right after her death, the rest of the family had left everything behind and gone into exile to the mother country. Mireille's grandmother had completely lost her mind. In the course of her ten years in exile, she must have said two lines. For Mireille's mother, exile had been considerably less dramatic than the emotional wound she had suffered. Her permanent discomfort had slowly gnawed away at her zest for life. In truth, her personal destruction dated much further back. It had begun on her eleventh birthday, when her father, a member of a small group ready to kill and die for French Algeria, had started to visit her bedroom regularly and force her to accept a cruel expression of love in the form of incest.

She met her husband in a repatriation camp in the South of France. He was drawn to her reserved and submissive demeanor. Their mutual sadness was shared in silence and great restraint. He was a hardworking workaholic; she was serious and self-effacing. Even with little dialogue, they had managed to live pretty well. He had found the ideal job for his silence and misanthropy as a truck driver, gone for weeks at a time with nothing but the monotonous hum of the engine for company. To make ends meet, his wife became a cleaning lady, ironing, and at times helping families who could afford hired help with childcare. In spite of herself, she had found a way to move on discreetly and with great humility. This was basically how they had provided a decent childhood for their daughter. Every three years, Mireille had spent a month-long holiday in a camp, in the same place on the Mediterranean side. The family tragedies had taught them to save and always be prepared for hard times. That is why Mireille had grown up in an apartment with very little light and life, no music, no books, leaving aside the television programs, some advertisements and a few fashion magazines. It was only after she had left her home and living in university housing that her mother, in a convulsive state of panic, had finally relieved herself of the weight of her past by evoking some of the episodes that had completely turned her life upside down. She had become a virtuoso in the art of waiting around in silence.

For Mireille, her father was a strange body who happened to share the same home in which she lived. His sentences were almost inaudible, and the ideas he had about people dated back to the nineteenth century. There is no doubt that this is precisely what had encouraged her to create the imaginary world she was so excited to share with Drissa and me. This also explained her incredible admiration for the extravagant stories the ancestor told and the ramblings from Drissa's uncle.

Mireille's parents sincerely liked Black people. They are kind and harmless, her father would say, when we were children. Even to this day, her mother is very polite with my mother. I want to believe that over the years they have come to share a kind of mutual affection even if it has never prompted them to confide in each other. There is something still that keeps them apart. I always had the feeling that Mireille's mother had guessed very early on that there was something between her daughter and me. A mother can sense these things. But she had never spoken up about it. Maybe she took pleasure in imagining that her daughter allowed herself to be happy, allowed herself a little bit of fantasy. She and her husband had tolerated our friendship while we were kids, but once we became adults and they saw signs of us getting serious, they worked to slowly undermine our relationship and in the end they succeeded.

Today, above all else, Mireille considers herself Jewish. Cut out your childish nonsense, she would say in her facial expression, falcons are domesticated worse than dogs in the Saudi Arabian desert. There are all these incredible things happening to our planet and you don't even realize it. It's in danger. What state are we going to leave it in for our children? Be serious. All you ever think about is fucking. Stop feeling me up all the time. It's annoying. Stop being so superficial. Grow up. We have to get informed, get involved in the fight. Cowing down in my chair, I beg her to spare me her political combat, her student activism. Do I drive you crazy with all those African issues, AIDS, civil wars, the systematic raping of men and women, from the Atlantic all the way up to the Great Lakes? Genocides and mountains of hands without bodies in Sierra Leone? You don't even bother to stop by and check in on your friends in the neighborhood who are having a really hard time, and now you're going on about saving the planet. You hardly ever smile and your caresses are basically hard labor for you. She explained how it made her sad to see how much we had strayed away from our beautiful younger years. She was concerned for Drissa and me, especially Drissa, who wasn't doing so well, had a pretty screwed up vision about things if not to say horrific, drinking alcohol and getting wasted all the time, his speech, basically incomprehensible. . . . She couldn't stand him anymore. I made her uncomfortable. More and more, she wanted to be alone and then one day she just took off.

Drissa didn't get his high school diploma. A few weeks before the exam, he decided not to get out of bed. When the body is so heavy and numb, the outside world feels really threatening. When you have taken in so much, at some point you can't be bothered to fight anymore. And under the covers, it's warm and cozy. He created his very own sweet and safe alcove, listened to the radio while he caressed himself gently beneath the warm covers. I should have seen right then and there that he was falling apart.

So he didn't join us when we went on to study in Paris. I only bumped into him on the weekends from time to time. The only time we ever met up was in Paris, and I rarely saw Mireille in the neighborhood. Most people didn't even recognize her anymore. Who do you think you are? So you think you're better than us because you go to college in Paris? She was always strutting around with books by illustrious authors, banging on about all the great boulevards in the capital. Why didn't you come to Kamel's party the other night, you snubbing us now?

Poor Mireille, what were we really berating her for, wanting to live differently somewhere else, for trying to leave behind the trajectory of those who are always coming in last, who finish somewhere in the background? Eternal spectators, who give in to the will of others, with their envious gazes, insults ready at hand to be spouted out at those who do differently, hands tightly fisted and ready to hit someone. Those who hesitate and doubt themselves for so long, they wind up stuck in fear and boredom. Mireille wants to live a full and colorful life far from the shit between the national highway, the ugly buildings and the supermarket. She wants to get as far away as possible from all the gray, from the dilapidated human cages, from the spit and the smell of urine in the stairwells, where everything is dirty and half broken. Mireille just wants to experience life more fully, in her entire being, and not glued before a television screen looking on at it and dreaming about it from the outside. She wanted to be smack in the middle of life while it's happening. She wanted to meet people who were doing extraordinary things with their lives, like in those stories you hear about, hanging on practically to every word, hungry to discover what happens next in their remarkable lives. Mireille had to really have the courage of her convictions because we don't care much for those who have visions of a better life, who want to live differently from the rest of us. We'd prefer they stayed close, no matter how painful it may be, rather than have to watch them all happy, having realized great achievements and living far away from us!

In my dreams and my brief intense romance, Mireille is elegant and full of life. Flying above cities and then sadly her feet suddenly become heavy. She struggles to stay air-borne and then thousands of hands with sharp nails try to hold her back and prevent the slightest movement on her part, halt her desire to defy the angels. Then, a loud noise, the sound of thunder, and when I wake up, I'm mad at myself for failing to understand her. I had to go through steel and subject my body, my mind, and my spirit to complete failure. Freedom Mireille, the world has opened its arms to you. Mireille dared to go beyond her doubts, make that great leap and outsmart her fears and anxieties. I hope she celebrates her courage day and night, and that she will flourish in life.

On Sunday nights, once back at the university dormitory, Mireille would soak in a warm, disinfectant bath, scrub herself intensely to remove the smells, the noise, the words, and the faces of what used to be her home. Most likely she would have disowned me if she had heard about my downfall, sitting here in a dark cell.

Bad luck is an infectious malady. It has a tenacious odor that can easily take up residence in the soul. She would have said to herself, look at what I might have become, ashamed and beaten. I wouldn't have known what to say, I would have simply lowered my head and my eyes, swallowed my pain in a sigh. Suck it up, the world is yours for the taking!

—⁂—

Mireille and I wanted to keep our promise no matter what, so after high school we had decided to travel all over Europe together for four weeks. Out of respect, we hadn't said anything to Drissa, who, in any event, had all sorts of excuses to avoid us. I was lucky enough to land a job with a businessman who was a friend of Kamel's and so I was able to earn some money for our trip. After three years spent in

prison and added time for getting involved in some serious drug trafficking, Kamel, formerly known as Dinosaur, was now proud to play
big brother according to the strict precepts of the Islamic faith. He'd
been sentenced after getting involved in some pretty serious armed
robbery stuff involving hostages, and so his police friends, who had
otherwise covered him with the drug trafficking crimes, could only
get his sentence reduced. Now I've known Kamel since we were kids
and so I could tell from the look on his face and by the way he carried
himself that he was really making an effort to show everyone that
he was a changed man. He worked really hard, and played mediator
in all kinds of disputes among the youth in the neighborhood. For
Kamel, respect was key. He was ready to fight long and hard to make
people forget his past.

He told me several times how much he regretted not getting his
diploma because he's sure it would have made his reconversion much
easier. He was conscious of the obstacles he faced in achieving the
complete transformation he hoped for. His teachers, when they
talked about him, had chills running down their spine. To them, he
was literally poison of the worst kind, violent and uncontrollable,
who couldn't even spell his own name right.

He was so glad to help me out whenever he could and to introduce
me to his new crew. He was genuinely emotional and happy when he
formally introduced me to his very first employers. I could feel how
much it meant to him, and he was so grateful.

His employers were a couple of low-key Jewish *pieds-noirs* who had
a stand in the town's market where they sold exotic dried fruit and
other products from the Mediterranean, twice a week. They didn't
want to know my name or learn anything about me. I showed up
one morning with Kamel; they barely explained what they expected
from me and didn't even take the time to really look at me or greet
me with a smile. They couldn't be bothered with common courtesy.
At the time, I had only one dream, to get on the train with Mireille
and take off with her on a real adventure, far away from everything.
Once she'd received sufficient financial allowances for her excel-

lent school results, we decided that we'd meet at the Gare de Lyon. Florence, Venice, Madrid, hello world, here we come!

Sitting in my present distress, I can still feel the intensity of that unbelievable moment of happiness. It was like a shot of freedom. The kind of feelings and ideas you dream about in the privacy of your bedroom or while strolling along the alleys in your neighborhood, but that you can barely imagine actually becoming a reality. Just like a cliché, we met up on the platform. I think she wanted it to be just like that. Me standing there waiting for her; she coming toward me. A little wave of the hand, and her running up to me and throwing herself into my arms as I spun her around in the air while she held on to her hat and kissed me fully on the lips, all smiles. She wore a simple white cotton dress, just below the knees and with lace straps, her feet light in her ballerinas. Dressed exactly like the woman in the TV commercial I like so very much. In the commercial, the woman runs into the water, takes three steps and then jumps and throws her hat high up into the sky.

On this day, Mireille was that image! She was the princess of my days and hot wild nights!

We had so many loving words for each other during our trip to Italy. We started the trip by way of Paris, went through the suburbs, the RER train stations, past the gray dismal-looking buildings of the housing projects, sad and dirty, and then finally into the countryside. Far away from everything, it was just the two of us and silence. We were happy, her thick curly black hair laying on my chest, smiling, her lips on my skin. She was into me. I was her country. By dawn, we were in Italy, the freshness of the summer morning made us shiver a bit. A whole new décor, the air delightfully perfumed. The instructions from the immigration officers were music to the ear, Mireille's face expressed relief. She looked on at me to see if I had realized that I was now really far away from everything. She stretched her body and laughed, relieved. We were in Florence. It was six o'clock in the

morning. The city was still asleep. We wanted to take advantage of
the deserted streets and avoid the naïve and sordid hordes of tourists.

She had spoken to me many times about the Florence syndrome.
The remarkable beauty of the place would make any charmed traveler experience a terrible malaise, especially standing in the piazza
Stendhal had written so much about and made infamous. We found
it yesterday when we crossed the famous bridge. The city square is so
narrow and the palace is so high up, but to be honest, we were so intoxicated and overwhelmed by our feelings that she literally passed
out in my arms. Mireille, what pleasure to feel you so close to me, to
feel your whole body vibrating as you abandoned yourself into my
arms. I savor this moment with the certainty that loving someone is
the one truth in this world.

Then Venice, Mireille and I gliding through the maze of the canals,
swimming at the Lido beach, just so we could say we had been there
at least once, later camping in Rome with the pleasure of making love
under the stars, and finally the Genoa train station that we wound
up missing, so caught up in our kissing. We stopped in Nice, another
childhood dream, lying on the pebble beach, without a single word,
our eyes looking up at the sky, overwhelmed by the feeling that we
were finally living. We went on to Seville. Spain in the summer heat,
thirty-six hours in the train without a shower, Mireille's scent was
so strong it made me crazy. Mireille, I wanted to take you then and
there!

Final stop, Portugal. Lost in Lisbon and its alleyways, we stop in a
tavern where Mireille drinks too much white wine. She has the modesty not to complain about our inevitable departure. Neither she nor
I express a single word of sadness or regret. We simply treasure our
final walk in a faraway country. Tipsy, she meanders along, a little
unsure of her footing on the steep paths. Alone in a city that has long
gone to sleep, we are gradually overcome by desire. Moaning, she
insists I make love to her right there and then, with her leaning up
against the wall. The autumn in her eyes stares intensely into mine.
We keep our clothes on, leaving the necessary space to explore the

rhythm of our bodies. Shivering as she holds me up against her in a mixture of pleasure and pain at not being able to swallow me up whole, her eyes open wide to the intensity of the pleasure. In this moment, everything becomes light and beautiful. At the height of our pleasure, I groan deeply, Mireille looks into my eyes and digs her fingers into my skin. Abandoning herself to what she's feeling, we finally hold each other. In the height of pleasure, Mireille's body twitches uncontrollably.

On the journey back to Paris in the train, we talked about future travels. Our next trip would be to Israel. You're so beautiful in your boundless joy. You know how to make dreams come alive. You're a new and unusual elixir, always so maddeningly measured, your hands in mine, with an insatiable passion. You're the one forging the key to our future. Jerusalem, culture and history to start things off, then on to Elath to relax and enjoy ourselves by the beach, one of her uncles lives in a kibbutz there where she plans to take me. She wants me to discover the land of her people. Later on, we will dive body and soul into the Bakongo country, under the protective eye of the invisible eternal leopards, sit at the tombs of our ancestor without fear of sorcerers or witch doctors. Knowing her childlike enthusiasm, I'm sure she'll love it. We could end our day lying on the white sandy beach at Pointe-Noire, listening to the sounds of the Atlantic Ocean. With the sky just above us, we could keep feeding our fantasies! The train continues in a monotonous hum, the countryside under an incredible heat wave, and the hideous buildings soon consume the horizon before us. From our window, we see commuters climbing mechanically into the RER. Then come the roofs and the noisy streets of Paris, while Mireille and I sleep, wrapped up in each other, peacefully.

—∞—

How could you have forgotten the intensity of our nights together, Mireille, the peaceful sleep, my head against your chest? Is this really what you're now calling stories about kids? Remember the night Kamel stole the blue car with the big engine. Drissa and I were used to taking the RER to go to parties, but Kamel was showing off about his new invention taxi-débrouille. You want to go somewhere, just find a ride down the road, and then you pretty much take off. You know, it's kind of like a mini-loan. Long live solidarity! He laughs, revealing the few teeth he has left, and before you know it we're off for a night out on town.

Nine miles down the highway, Bob Marley blasting through the speakers, the owner of the car has some good tunes, Kamel driving still with no license, he never got the code so he could pick one up in the bureau; Drissa, up front, scared for his life; and me, hanging out in the back seat wondering if Mireille will hook up with us. We were going so fast that the trees on the sidewalk seemed to form a straight line. Kamel and Drissa realized I wasn't in the mood to talk or mess around. Drissa was listening to Kamel tell him that they'd finally found his sister who'd run away. Kamel's mother had given him the privilege of lacerating the offender so that she would forever wear the unforgiveable scars of her moral degradation. One more reason for Drissa's descent into insanity, his captivity in silence. What is the best part of man? I am one with the reggae music and I open up a bottle of gin. Up in the front of the car, dead silence, the end of that tragic story left a chill in the air. Drissa would like to exit for another life, slip into another skin; Kamel isn't quite sure anymore of the difference between good and evil. He recalls the games he used to play with his sister when they were kids but very quickly returns to his mask of the fierce brute, ready to take on the whole world if he has to. It's a huge relief when he finally parks in front of the entrance to the party. After all it's Saturday night, it's time to have some fun. We greet our friends, shake a few hands here, four kisses there, this is Kamel's crowd and he's back in his element as the big boss man; Drissa, the dark mysterious silent one, clueless when it comes to relaxing and being lighthearted; and then there's me, practically drunk and pretty much feeling hopeless. I get the feeling that she's not going to come. Ludovic was also there, dancing like a crazy man on the huge dance floor.

Mireille did finally show up with her friend Carole while Drissa was helping me between tears and vomiting. After being so gentle and taking really good care of me, he explained to Mireille how much I'd missed her. Mireille stood there torn between wanting to go have a good time on the dance floor and a sense of duty to stay and take care of me. Mireille, light of my life, you knew how to use just the right tone to talk to me. We sat together at the foot of a tree in the night, the sound of your voice lulling me, while you soothed me by caressing the nape of my neck. My head on your thighs, I was virtually drowning in the universe between your legs. Drissa and Carole had hooked up with the others for some time now when suddenly chairs started flying around the bar area. Mireille was telling me that they'd had to hitchhike to get here and that a fascist pig in a red and white car had picked them up. He was a student officer, on his way to visit his grandmother not far from the dance hall. He would have been glad to give them a ride home but was too afraid of these kinds of parties. She always knew how to temper my jealousy. With a reassuring smile, I kissed her inner thighs, her dress was a bit rolled up and with my teeth I freed her from her undergarment. A bit embarrassed at first, she laughed and then took a deep breath once my mouth touched her thick and tender skin. With the juices from her adorable garden on my lips and tongue I tasted the spice of lovers.

Hidden in the darkness about some sixty feet away from the dance hall, we had missed the beginning of the fighting. All of a sudden people were rushing outside, tear gas had been sprayed, some people were screaming, others were crying. A huge brawl was going on in mass confusion. By some sheer miracle, Drissa and Kamel found us. We had to get out of there as fast as we could! Two CRS police vans had already turned up, loaded with clubs, boots, and helmets. Those who were jumping like crazy on top of cars or running around not knowing what to do were among the first to get caught.

Drissa gave us one of those warm, almost paternal looks, like you would give a baby who was just having a good time, not making any trouble. He thanked Mireille. Kamel couldn't contain his excitement. For him a night out without a fight was not a real night out. He managed to land a couple of punches and get away from the police. Luckily Mireille recognized the student officer's car that had picked her up earlier in the evening, which made Kamel overjoyed. There's nothing quite like stealing the car of a son of a bitch, future representative of law and order, to make a Saturday night out really special. He promised to bang it up pretty good once he got it back to the neighborhood.

Back on the highway in the dark of the night, the same trees but in the opposite direction and this time no music. On the back seat, Mireille and I were wrapped up in each other, tighter than ever, the palm of my hand crushed under the volume of her bare curves, my fingers inside her, drowning in pleasure. She was biting her hand to stop herself from screaming out her pleasure. Drissa, serious and brooding, listened to Kamel explain how angry he was that he'd never set foot in Algeria and yet his father had fought on behalf of France during the war. No one could give a shit. For the French, he's just another brown-skinned, frizzy-haired guy. An Arab. For others, he was the son of a traitor. The more he talked, the worse his driving became. The car was going to be a way to avenge himself. Once we arrived, I asked him to loan me the car for an hour and then he would have all the time in the world to destroy it. He wished us a good fuck and took off grinning with Drissa.

Waking out of her drowsiness, Mireille started on Kamel, criticizing his attitude, his way of speaking, she's had enough of hanging out with guys like him! But it must have been written somewhere that that night was ours. For I had no problem taking her home. Oh Mireille, in the quiet of the night, our kisses were each time more intense, hands all over the body, liquid desire, you undressed me, possessed by an aching hunger for pleasure that had to be satisfied. Her skirt pulled far up on her stomach, Mireille melts into love and holds me tight. Confined in the car, overwhelmed by desire, the culmination of our union, it was our very first time!

On the vacant lot, Kamel kept rolling his joint while he asked Drissa why he'd had an argument with Carole. Drissa should not have let her take off with that son of a bitch Ludovic. All Drissa had to do was say the word and he'd go right over and beat the shit out of him. The only response Drissa had was to get high, take a long puff that kept him propelling far away up into the gentle, peaceful night air, a sensation of warmth and lightness, an ephemeral but absolutely reassuring caress. They found a sort of communion in the crackling of the marijuana as it continued to burn out as they passed it back and forth between them. The body releases, relaxes, softens, thousands of images of happiness and simplicity flood the mind. Time passes easily and life finally feels good.

Mireille invited me inside her, guided me with her hands resting on the small of my back. At first I let her set the rhythm of my movements. Once the pain had passed, she let herself go completely. I stripped her and made passionate love to her. She sat on the back seat with me in front of her, almost standing in the middle of her body, my hands stuck to the speakers, my chest on her face, distorted from all the convulsions and panting. The cramped space of the car yielded the sunniest meadow.

Kamel and Drissa were no longer talking on the vacant lot. They'd stretched out, just letting their salutary hallucination run its course from head to toe, a wild feeling in the night, nothing else existed, blood and bones were forgotten, had melted away, and a beautiful light embraced the whole area. There was no more country, no past, no future. They just simply felt really good.

A minute, an hour or more, perhaps less, time no longer mattered. Barely coming down off his trip, Kamel decided it was time to take care of the fucking cop car, but Drissa could no longer hear him, he was on his own planet, a big smile on his face.

Fast asleep, Mireille was holding me tight against her chest when Kamel approached us. She'd asked me not to pull out. I was enjoying the pleasure of feeling her body loosening up. She held me for a long

time in her arms, maternally, sighing deeply, alternating kisses with
gentle caresses of my hair. We'd barely fallen asleep when Kamel surprised us. Hey love birds, I've got work to do! He had the decency to
step away so that we could quickly get dressed, still intoxicated from
our lovemaking. Our first time was so beautiful that we never spoke
about it. Words can so easily spoil what belongs only in memory.

Mireille, my darling, my love, my peace, this irreplaceable magic,
when I'm dozing off, my face against your breast.

—∞—

My sleep is disturbed by loud bangs and faraway screams that
gradually come closer and eventually surprise me. Earlier, I heard
the dreadful howling of a desperate woman. She was screaming hys-
terically, refusing to believe that her husband had left her. Where had
he gone? What will become of their little Marie? She's going to wait
for him no matter what. This is all just a nightmare, a bad joke. She
insists that someone take a phone and call him right away! Other
tremulous voices try to console her, they are truly sorry. Some even
join her in her sobbing. I imagine her struggling, stuck in some kind
of a trance. I would love for her to come and join me in my hole so
we can share our pain. She's looking for the son-of-a-bitch, the real
piece of shit that he is. You have to be a real monster to do something
like that, and since I understand her all too well, let me be the one to
call for help, so that they can free me and put an end to the injustice
and reign of these ferocious beasts. She's screaming at the top of her
lungs, and I'm going out of my mind in my cell. Our mutual distress
forms a singular disturbing body. Madam, I don't know you but I
feel as though I already love you. We're already joined together for
eternity in this revolt of those skinned-alive, confined to a life of in-
comprehension that we have had to give up on, accept to never know
who we are, and never truly understand the meaning of our actions.
You're already crying for the life you had with your husband and that
you now have to mourn. I have also lost. The anguish of absence.

A few minutes later, a deafening blow to the body followed by the
sound of a bone snapping. It's me that they're beating. Let me sleep

and remember. I'm so exhausted. It feels like a bunch of them are hitting me and roughing me up; or are some of them actually trying to protect me? It's a ballet of confusion between the uniforms, all the insults, the calls to order. Murderer, he was a family man, he left behind a wife, a young baby who will never know him, all because of you, we're going to crush you and bleed you dry like a pig.

I can also sing songs, blues filled with gallons of broken hearts. If you took the time to listen to me just for one minute, I could mesmerize you with funeral tunes that would make your soul cry.

I'm like a boat caught in a storm, my body at the mercy of forces greater than me. They're dragging me all over the place, to the right, to the left, up, and down. Stop. Let the courts do their job. Strangely enough, I don't feel any pain. I kind of like these sudden chaotic moves, they lull me in their own unique way. I get to escape from everything.

I enter into the body of the ancestors, when as a child, one morning I almost drowned in the turbulent waters of the Congo River. I suddenly found myself surrounded by this fierce, uncontrollable body of liquid, torturing and consoling me all at the same time, a warm and bitter sensation, torrid and deadly. My eyes keep opening and closing, frightened at the lure of the void. Life is so ludicrous that I sometimes wish it could just be over, I could take off for a whole new experience, head toward the end and finally rid myself of all this dead weight. The problem is I'm actually afraid to leave it all behind.

Once, when they were swimming among friends, the ancestor decided to take the challenge out of sheer bravado and dive into the capricious and dangerous waters. A group of about six or seven cheerful boys who'd been playing and had gotten all hot and sweaty, and one of them suggested they all go swimming. No one wanted to admit that they were afraid of the river; the fact that it was prohibited was enough to motivate them. Some of them jumped in right away. The ancestor was among the last ones to get into the thick liquid green mass. The idea was to swim against the current for about ten meters and meet up by the floating weeds. The bravest among them had already come to the surface and started to tease him. Further downstream, the rapids were dangerously rumbling their call, or might it have been the cry of those who had drowned, all of those souls forever detained in the intricate winding paths of the rocks?

Watch out, they whispered. He had now gone beyond the view of the riverbank. The red and black sky became his universe; deadly fright his only companion. He was swimming and drowning, abandoned to the capricious and hazardous temperament of the waters. He was getting tired, his screams stifled among the enormous bubbles. The hand of death held him in its grip. Disoriented, he gave up all hope. The course of the river was about to triumph.

This aquatic journey lasted a few minutes, ebbing and flowing between the visible and invisible worlds. At times, he was a prisoner ready to return to the great universe of those spirits who had gone on before. At other times, when his head came up above water, he had a chance to fill up his lungs with vital oxygen, nourish himself with the light of day, scream, and call out for help. Standing on the bank of the river, the boys who finally realized the impending disaster did not hesitate to take off as fast as their legs could carry them.

The ancestor had no difficulty recognizing the beauty of a life well led, a life of peace and calm, filled with mystical beings. A universe of peace, fairness, and serenity. During this perilous journey, the fragility of men, their multiple essences came before him in the form of a mysterious figure, an image worn by time. A sign from above, he was fighting so that his eyes and the meaning of the message in his gaze could conquer the flow of the currents. An old man, whose hair had turned white over time, was supporting him. Barely able to hold himself upright but determined on maintaining his dignity with the help of a cane, this man implored the dead to leave him to continue on with his life. In that very moment, he was named a herald so that he could wear, alongside his flesh and his blood as a man, the breath of the leopard under his skin.

I'm drowning and reviving over yonder. Everything is getting mixed up again, the water coming downstream from the cascade, the brawl that my head, my arms, and my legs are having a hard time taking refuge from. I'm just letting myself go. Flow, pain, I'm opening my arms up to you, bring me days of hope. At that moment, a branch falls right into the palm of my hand, I cling to it, a miracle has happened. The departure that I'd finally accepted is receding and I can now gather up whatever strength I have left to courageously drag myself over to the roots, solidly planted at the riverbank hundreds of years ago. I can hear a melancholic farewell song rising up from the depths of the rapids. The heart of the shipwrecked victims has brought me back to life. They are watching over me while I doze off, after having cried for so long over my unforgettable pain and anguish. I'm in turmoil. I've been in a thunderstorm for generations, it's written on my body. Finally I can sleep soundly.

I can remember my first steps on French soil. I was so enchanted. It was the month of January. That very first leap of a child coming out of the airplane and my disappointment when I realized that in the world I had dreamed about for so long, it was raining, cold bad weather, gray skies, punctuated by disturbing mechanical sounds. I'd imagined a gentle sun, a wonderland, covered by an immense glass dome under which White people ran around, living together in harmony. I'd imagined that they had succeeded in creating a world of profound humanity, alleviated of most material preoccupations.

Almost immediately, I was greeted by the harshness of the cold. It gripped me in the face, froze my fingers with a stinging sensation, all terribly painful, a horrible surprise when I opened my luggage. There I was, a shocked, whining child. I lost my way trying to get back home. Since that time, I have slowly settled into jails of differences.

What are you? Chinese? I smile with my old fear of light-colored blue eyes, they remind me of raw flesh, not to speak of that angular nose, pointed like the arrows of warriors on the day of the parade celebrating Independence. As a child, I was always immensely sad to see these people condemned to suffer just so they could breathe like the rest of us. Luckily Mireille was there, sitting next to me in kindergarten. She would grab my hand that was clinging tightly to

our teacher's hand. Together we would pace up and down in the
courtyard.

Amazing Mireille. She instinctively understood the pain of exile,
and yet we were only five years old! She would wear short "little girl"
dresses, and I never missed an opportunity to notice her poorly fitted
white cotton panties that left her pink buttocks exposed. Mireille
also came to my rescue during the *galette des rois* cake celebration.[2]
I had no idea what was going on, neither the language nor the tradi-
tion. I had bitten into the bean and they all screamed in chorus, it's
him, he has it, he has it! Enthusiasm and reproach can get mixed up
in the mind of a person who doesn't know what's going on. I started
crying my heart out. Mireille cleverly positioned herself with au-
thority right next to me and passed her frail arms around my waist.
She was my queen right from the beginning, my personal savior in
adversity.

School is important! The words of the ancestor kept resonating in
my tiny chest to the point that I couldn't stop stumbling. Don't forget
that this is not your home. You have the burden of being a foreigner.
You have to be better than the White man otherwise he'll hate you.
Luckily, Mireille's little hand was there to hold mine, swinging it
joyfully up and down. She gave me blue, green, and so many tons of
red to have the courage to withstand so much.

—◊◊◊—

Go to sleep now; try to get some rest. The only prison you need be
afraid of is the one you enclose yourself in everyday, the one where
you are the prison guard. Forget about the bricks, the cement, and
the steel. Leave your blood and tears on the metal bars and lie down

---

2. The *galette des rois* is a flaked pastry cake traditionally on sale in France in
early January to celebrate Epiphany. A small bean or porcelain figure, known as a
fève, is inserted into the cake and the person who bites into it is anointed king (or
queen), gets to wear the golden paper crown that is sold with the cake, and then
select his queen (or her king) for the day.

in the filth on the ground. Stay on course and follow me. Remember to keep your heart and soul open!

As your uncle, I went looking for your father in the jungle where he was born. Our stubborn mother had left the convent and all those overly affectionate priests. She had been living among them against her will and one day finally took off with her uncles and the rest of the family. This all happened during colonization. These crazy men defied the authorities, burnt their identity papers, dared to look the White men in the eyes and risk imprisonment. After that they had to leave, otherwise things would have certainly gotten worse. So they went far away, into the heart of the jungle and back to our first village. A few huts made from wood, clay, and leaves; some indolent domesticated animals; and in the main square a mobongui fire. The fire, I love it too, this is our soul, it's the best moment of the day and of life, when the day is over and we gather around the homefire.

As you know, your father and grandmother didn't live in the village; they were living in the clearing, a mile or so away. When night falls and darkness colors the sky, you can close your eyes in your hut until morning. Your spirit brings you closer to the others who are dancing when the lights go out. They watch over us, and the mobongui. Your grandmother admitted to me, somewhat concerned, that your father really enjoyed staying up at night. Seated with his hands on his knees, you could watch him leaning to the left, then to the right, but more often than not, turned toward the sky. He wanted to immerse himself in the black light and become one with it and its angels. Shortly after surprising him in this way, our mother's companion disappeared forever, which confirmed the suspicions that had been made about him. He was accused of being a boa-man after his very own brother had caught him copulating with an enormous serpent. He tried to suggest that he had been the victim of an animal attack, but no one believed him, especially because his younger brother and the two old women who saw him at the time had immediately gone into a trance that lasted for hours. The poor soul had to resign from his position as deputy mayor of the small municipality in which he had been otherwise prospering. It's true that a boa-man can stir up a lot of fear and even fall victim to lynching the moment a baby or a young child shows signs of suffering from a persistent fever. Days went by peacefully in the clearing before they found him, his stepson barely a few years old by then, conversing naked and happy with the invisible in the pitch-black night, no sound, and no moon. Listen to your fatigue, calm down, and let the words flow.

I never quite understood your father's love for the invisible world. As a child, he was so inspired he would go on about it for hours. I don't think he ever even realized that most people are just content with what they can see and hold firmly in their hands. It's hard to believe that such a spiritual boy had welcomed me with a good pelting of stones. He was and always will be as wild as a baboon.

Everybody ran for cover whenever he came upon a white priest. You can understand why the other kids saw him as a country boy when I brought him to the capital at your grandmother's request so that he wouldn't grow up like an animal. Like our mother, he couldn't bear the injustices in the colonial world. Men in chains, standing single-filed in the streets for failing to pay taxes, and especially the intransigence and brutality of the militiamen who came from all corners of the colonial empire. These militias were composed of strong men who guaranteed the security of the evangelizing commandos in the countryside. At the crack of dawn, they would wake up the whole village to the sound of the Bible and for those who didn't like it, they would happily strike them with the buttstock of a rifle. These soldiers made up for their poor mastery of French with the whip and reserved the same treatment for the men and the women. They must have been handpicked for their stupidity and aggression. During interrogations, they were always sounding off viciously, beating while spitting out army life's some serio's shit!

The separation between black and white neighborhoods particularly outraged your father. Aside from his years spent in the clearing and the darkness of night, he'd also learned to read the books of White men and had come to realize a lot of things. For example, he wondered why the white neighborhoods were off-limits to the black population after dark in what was a Black country. At the hour that the siren sounded for civilization it was also chiming in terror in the capital. During this time, a story was circulating about a young student who had just returned from Paris. He was claiming that the Whites over there served him every day in cafés and restaurants, greeting him with *What can I get for you, Sir,* and welcoming him in their establishments. He took a good beating for this to teach him not to spread ridiculous lies. Just because he'd been away studying in France was no reason to come back with tall tales and take people for simple idiots willing to believe anything.

To calm his rage and indignation, your father focused on being the best in his class, and went on to become an important patriotic activist for independence, and even a freedom fighter for black people the world over. I have come to believe that he was never as happy as during those weeks of the nationalist liberation and jubilation when colonial rule finally came to an end. During that period, the nocturnal flights to the land of those-who-have-left-their-bodies-behind took second place to the changing realities of the time.

Those years will always be a source of great pride for him but sadly not of peace. Neither your father nor I could have imagined the violence that would persist, the arbitrary governance that became the order of the day, and the corruption that came to eat at the very fabric of the society. We naively rushed headfirst into the socialist farce. "Everything for the people, nothing but the people." Hearing this slogan during one of our meetings, an old man, with a kind of botched up French, somewhat confused, asked us in our own language why was there in fact nothing for the people in this revolution and instead a bunch of weapons in the barracks. The leader of our proletarian revolution immediately squelched this bourgeois-reaction-of-an-imperialist-conspiracy-sort-of-valet-to-capitalism. We taught him the Marxist-Leninist principles Kalashnikov-style, and we certainly didn't forget to carry out an in-depth frisking under the loincloths his wife and daughters wore. Consistent with the

revolutionary principles, his sons were given a thorough beating and
incarcerated with him. Army life's some serio's shit!

Given all the injuries he sustained, he was basically handicapped
for life. He was only released from prison once he'd sworn on the
Bible that he would agree to the marriage between his youngest
daughter and the friend of the head of the police in the district, a
sixty-year-old guy, local general secretary of the one-party government, a mass movement that promised to bring light to the people,
blah, blah, blah. . . . The general secretary already counted three
wives, half a dozen official mistresses and legitimized his children
through a distribution system of local game.

You were born around this time, at what ended up being the most
maternal phase of Modern Africa. Africa was in the hands of the
Chinese who were convinced of the Maoist revolution and seduced
by the idea that the new man could be created by hard work. They
were highly qualified, always pleasant, and willing to help. They believed in their mission so much so that it wasn't surprising to hear
them speaking French, Lingala, or Kikongo. Okay, so their accent
wasn't always the best, but we had the greatest admiration for their
level of commitment. One of them, the doctor who delivered you,
even became friends with your father. You could never tell his age,
and he had a name that was impossible for a Bantu to pronounce,
but he came around regularly to check up on you, always bearing
gifts from his country. We'd never come across someone so simple and polite, especially because many of your father's Congolese
colleagues, from the moment they received their student card for
a European university, would undergo a complete transformation,
turning into these high-minded and haughty authoritarian puppets.
The friendship with this Chinese man was strange all the same because even though he was quite generous himself, he never accepted
anything from your father, not even the simple pleasure of sharing
a meal. Party orders? Who knows? Let's face it; fraternity among
countries clearly has its limits. When all is said and done, when it

comes time to belting out a tune, we all have our different rhythms and melodies, whether in Beijing, Moscow, Brazzaville, or Paris.

Besides the Chinese delegation responsible for building bridges, roads, and hospitals, we also had Cuban militia and East German henchmen in place to ensure the quality of our security services. There were French overseas volunteers to guarantee a rational school education and to promote French-language usage at the equator, as well as special envoys from the Vatican sporting black frocks, guardians of the African soul. They made it very clear that given the current state of affairs, the autochthon was far more in need of catechism than mathematics, and that it was important to learn to prioritize! The sovereign, independent nation to which freedom had been generously granted now found itself once again in good hands. First, we learned to ask for things, then we protested for what was rightfully ours, and today we've succeeded in becoming a nation of panhandlers, plaintiffs, our hands always outstretched and our bellies perpetually empty. Sad eyes turned toward the sky because salvation comes in the form of a cargo aircraft filled with medication and food or celestial blessings.

Caught up in the flurry of the intermingling of different nations, inspired by the many people originating from faraway lands, your father quickly caught the travel bug and sought out new places to which he could bring his language, his history, his knowledge, as well as that of his beloved people. He also wanted you to be rid of inhibitions and discover the world in all its diversity. He therefore prepared your departure for France with great enthusiasm. The world was yours for the taking.

Get some more rest now. Don't start kowtowing . . .

—ᴨᴠ—

In the quiet and calm, I'm still able to find refuge in the lingering effects of the alcohol and marijuana. My quarters of fortune are filthy, and it's dark. A few square feet of floor space in which to find myself face to face with myself, with a story to write and most of the pages still practically blank. In my turmoil, I just pissed on myself. The warden is cracking up like a whale behind the door. He must have got a whiff of the odor. I have to admit that this warm sensation is the one pleasant thing that has happened to me in these last hours. I better savor it before I have to deal with the discomfort of wet clothing on my skin and the nauseating stench drowning my nostrils.

With all this fear and misunderstanding, I'm longing to put my anxieties to bed and accept whatever help I can get. I'm in severe pain, it's so diffuse that I can't quite pinpoint it. Every body part, every inch of my body, my skin, organs, all together are unleashing their own dose of torture, without the slightest interruption so that I can get a little bit of relief. The cell is ridiculously small. I can't even stretch out my arms the width of the space. There isn't even a ray of light, not a single sound around me. My body is basically drowning in oblivion. For about fifteen minutes, I started to distract myself by hiding under the wooden bed, but that just really irritated the shit out of the guard on his rounds. I'd robbed him of a couple seconds of daylight. Panicked, he was looking for me in every little nook and cranny. What difference is it to him whether I'm on or under the bed? Just for that he'd felt the need to bang me about, his way of exorcising the fright I'd given him by disappearing in my own dungeon. Today, he was supposed to have gone to the bank and picked up the dry-cleaning. Don't lose your shit. Just relax. You're all protected behind your double metal doors, bars, and your locks and bolts.

I'm just letting the events of the past dance around in a frenzy. Many satellites are orbiting around me. They'd better keep their distance. I'm gladly hiding and pretending to be absent when they call my name. I'm just a spectator. Go ahead without me. I'm still watching. I need more time to fall in line. Excuse me. Can you cut me a little slack, please! Guilty or not, I'm the victim here. Me! A decision is going to be coming down from the captain by way of the ancestor, Mireille, and Drissa. I keep forgetting that I'm the only one who's going to have to answer to my hands, to my legs, to my fucked-up state, to my joy, to my sadness. For the moment, there is this peaceful distance between the world and me. Someone else is in charge of my fate. I can finally go to sleep without fear. Days will go by and with them beautiful images of both good times and failures. Give me the tranquilizer you give to the tamed animals. They don't bite anymore; they just sit there staring at you, wisely waiting before their trough. Three meals per day, a walk so I don't forget what fresh air is and bars to make it absolutely clear where the boundaries are.

I get recurring visions of an irreparable catastrophe, I'm running, trying to get away, I stumble and then suddenly nosedive into a bottomless pit. The fall makes me really anxious and gives me a chill worse than this icebox prison cell. I keep trying to reassure myself when I finally regain my composure, only there is nothing, no right side, no flipside, no right, no wrong.

I feel like screaming or crying when I realize that all the hours I'm in here rotting away, my poor little cat has been all alone in my room, the poor thing must be meowing, afraid, and dying of hungry. In the end, he's not that different from me, sitting around waiting, no clue whatsoever about what's going on.

One can only hope all this is some terrible misunderstanding. The door could open at any given moment and a familiar face, perhaps the red confused face of the captain, would be standing right by me. I'll accept his apology of course, no hard feelings man, a nice long shower and let's forget all about it. One or two steps back into the past, leave behind Drissa, Mireille, the questions and all this sticky mess I got mired in on the left sidewalk, a complete one-eighty and I'm good to go.

I'll breathe again, glad to have escaped a close call. I'll realize that life is beautiful for those who've escaped the worst. I'll take a stroll and take in life in all its beauty, come shy of giving myself a cricked neck from turning my head to look at all those fine ladies in Saint-Germain. Relaxed, I'll be able to enjoy a nice cold brew on the terrace of one of the chicest cafés. All smiles. Cigarette in the mouth, hello, may I sit with you. By the end of the day, I'll buy a ticket at the Gare de Lyon, mainline train, sleep in a compartment all alone with a dream girl, wake up to an amazing view of the Mediterranean, right there smack in front of you. All nice and clean, I'm looking good at the beach. The light is so bright, it almost blinds me, or could it be that girl, the most beautiful girl in the world that I want to get to know? She's already smitten with me, thinks I'm amazing, handsome, intelligent. I take my shoes off. I'm wearing light, summer clothes. A cloud comes over me. We understand each other without needing to say a single word. The wind, the sea, we have all the time in the world to kiss each other. The entire beach is just for the two of us. She soothes me with caresses. The skin of her fingers is so gentle, velvety. Her gestures feel good to the touch, stroking my body. There are birds up in the blue sky and boats out at sea. Somewhere at the tip of the horizon, far in the distance, sadly, the door still won't open.

Some feelings don't deceive. My ears are ringing. Within seconds my whole head is starting to vibrate. Someone from far away is trying to warn me. The message seems to be extremely serious. I'd better gather up all my strength because something has happened, and I'm nearing the point of no return. What if I'd really committed a crime, some abominable, horrific, irreparable act? Or if I'd been an evil bird, who brought misfortune, sadness, and distress into the lives of men? My body is starting to shiver from fear. Having shed their tears, an interminable procession of benevolent spirits starts to recede into the distance, turning their back on me. I've become a wild beast, ignoble, a hyena, eyes skewed, lurking around a carcass, swarmed by flies, vultures, jackals, and worms. I'm already falling apart under the weight of questions that are going to be coming at me. In my defense, I'm going to say that I just can't handle this life. I'm sorry for what I might have done; I have not been doing well lately.

—⁂—

So here we are finally, Mr. Captain, all alone, you and I, face to face. You would think that I missed you. I can see that you feel more secure now that I'm no longer a threat to you, handcuffed to a radiator hose on the ground. Complete subjugation, I don't even have the right to sit in front of you on a chair. Humiliated. Completely at your mercy. Half-naked. Within just a few hours, they've managed to turn me into a complete wreck. I'm basically getting used to this filth. My ass is completely exposed, and I can't even pull up my pants. This is clearly a case of miscarriage of justice. I've been reduced to shamelessly begging for a glass of water that they refused in an outburst of laughter. Believe me, even though I'm not so clear in my head right now, I am furious for giving you the pleasure of this image you have of me. If I were you, I wouldn't be so quick to rejoice. You should know that I've come a long way, and we're just getting started!

You're quite right officer, life in concrete jungle didn't really help. I never really learnt to feel my pulse beating in my arteries. I remember the boredom, the everyday mini dramas you get used to despite everything. We would meet up at the train station to hang out together. Everything is so sad and silent around us in fall and winter, and then total boredom in summertime, killing time at the local youth center just to piss off the deejay, smashing up telephone booths at night, putting out street lights with one well-calculated kick, smoking joints, and drinking cheap beer in the vacant lot or in the basement when it was raining. Idle, looking for any reason to pick a fight, insulting the petrified females going by, directing obscenities at them when they refused to talk to us.

Of course, I had Mireille and her books; she loved our endless discussions, the magic of the words and sentences that allowed us to travel together without it costing a penny. It was a great formula for feeding our dreams that lasted weeks at a time. When she spoke, her face was always beaming. She rarely mentioned her family or talked about herself, only about the cascades of verses and stanzas and pounds of prose that she wanted to share with me, during our walks together, sitting on a bench or sometimes on the ground, hand in hand. When the words were so beautiful and the meaning so infinitely profound, we would kiss each other even with our mouths full. We had always been so close that we were convinced that we'd found each other, as we say, for life. At this point in our adolescence, Drissa had already chosen a different path. Drissa, my brother, my friend, you have to cut it out, stop hitting that girl, she loves you, leave her alone. He sleeps with her as though he were masturbating with a porno magazine in the other hand. He insults her, you're nothing but a bitch dog, you bitch; he slaps her, kicks her in her sides. And yet she still keeps hanging on, begging him to come back to her. It's almost like she's herself again when she's by his side. She snuggles up right next to him, like a frightened little animal. Be careful, brother, the spirits don't forgive cruelty. They're all about benevolence and teaching us how to be generous. Watch out for a heart that turns bitter-homie! Stay alert. Stay attuned. Be on the lookout for vicious winds.

Shit, he throws his hand above his head, he's screaming, completely tone deaf. He can only see from one eye, the other eye is fixed on the basement. You're pissing me off with your whole bullshit about mystical signs, all that nonsense. It's primitive Banana nonsense that has never helped anyone. Just look around you, nothing has changed! Drissa sells stolen televisions and luxury items he's accumulated from all the robberies and drug sales. Now, I'm tttrripp-ping, bro; I'm a huge success, couldn't give a shit, go back to your yuppie-upper crust university with your little White girl. Who do you think you are? And who does she think she is showing contempt for me, as if she doesn't know me anymore, didn't we all grow up together? She can go fuck herself! Drissa, it's Mireille. Remember when we were kids, we were always hand in hand running around together on the vacant lot.

Be careful, Drissa, all the cruel words you throw out to hurt other people can wind up poisoning your own blood.

I'm making money now so I can shit on whatever I want. Please, leave me alone with all your bullshit, you're so naïve. While he's going on he's groping his girlfriend under her skirt and she's blushing. He pushes her violently to the ground and when she gets up, he grabs her crudely by the hair, get lost, you stupid bitch, hurry up. I know Carole; she's also from the neighborhood. She's slept with just about everybody. Her mother took off one day without leaving an address and never came back, tired of the daily beatings from her alcoholic husband. When we saw her everyday wearing her huge black sunglasses, we thought she was showing off. Some of us even called her Deneuve. Carole stayed and took care of her father who became stricken with grief and an even worse drunk. Those rare moments she had to herself she liked to spend them with Drissa whom she'd found so sweet and gentle ever since primary school when he was so cute, looking so lost, like someone who didn't even have a clue where he lived.

Now he beats her, hurts her, but never forgets her or leaves her. He's her one and only love, the only reason she has to keep going. She never ever wants to be without him. Not even madness could separate Drissa from Carole. She's filled with so much love and incredible tenderness that she radiates tremendous warmth and charm that make her irresistible. She had nothing to do with the ideal woman Drissa used to get all wet-dreamy about, but she had firmly secured her place in his life. She had a power over him that was borderline obsessive. Drissa couldn't stand next to Carole for more than an hour without getting flooded by a violent desire for her extremely feminine body, its smells and its curves, always ready to welcome him, not to mention her face beaming with pleasure, her lips pursed. He was crazy about her body. All his attempts to humiliate and hurt her only made his love for Carole greater, something he was never ever going to admit.

Submissive, she kneels before him. Disgusted, I take off. I'm her God, I can do whatever I want. His yelling and crazy laughter followed me all the way into the corridor. It still resonates within me to this day.

Be patient, captain, let me put things in the right chronological order, then I can give you all the confessions you need for your report and put your conscience to rest.

Drissa, my brother, my friend, always hanging around in these groups of rowdy young guys, impolite, vulgar, always aggressive among themselves and merciless with people they don't know. Settling scores, gun shots, one dead, another seriously injured, handicapped for life, gang rapes, barbaric acts, drug trafficking, police beatings in the neighborhood police station, joyrides, damages rising up to tens of thousands of Euros, multiple car thefts. The local schools have become incubators for delinquents, large-scale police operations, who combine merit badges with repeated cases of police misconduct.

You frighten everybody, Drissa, your mother, pedestrians, Mireille who used to be your friend. There are times you even dump your rage on me. You have to realize that, for us, you've always existed. In fact, we'd recognize you a lot better without this whole performance. We'd understand you so much more without all this freaky brouhaha you put on. All you're doing is making trouble in the streets, the train station, the RER, your life, your love. We only get a glimpse of you, make out the sound of a distant echo, without really getting to know you. Articulate, take a deep breath, choose your words carefully, one at a time, smile like you used to.

Drissa makes Carole sleep with other guys so that he can get a new CD player, a car radio, a little bit of hashish, insults, and beatings. Where is the deafness coming from that prevents you from realizing that you're already an important part of this world?

I could never truly be disgusted with Drissa or any of my friends from the neighborhood. I cherish the memories I have, the ever-present warmth of days and nights spent just being together, sharing a laugh, kicking back, and chilling. I would love to forget all that I've witnessed and learned and go back to the days of laughter, when there were no important decisions that had to be made, no stands that had to be taken. What if we just went over to the vacant lot and ran around till we were all out of breath like back when we were kids, or simply sat around at the entrance, sharing some cigarettes and the latest news about the football championship, talked about the new girl in the neighborhood, her chest, her face, her ass. When our lives started to change, Mireille could no longer tolerate the violence, the harshness, and the unhealthy environment, abominable in fact, into which many had fallen.

The last time she made an appearance in the neighborhood, she got into an argument with some of the guys who just killed time hanging out on a bench not far from the supermarket. Infuriated, she compared them to a bunch of pigs wallowing in their own shit, only good for terrorizing their own people and disappointing their mothers. Real losers, who had to get stoned to avoid looking each other directly in the face. Only the most brutal anger can let you forget the mistakes you try to hide from yourself because the truth is that they're torturing us all the time. You see yourself drifting on the road of no guts, no glory, and you keep on going, and somewhere along the way you just give up.

One of the guys answered her by making it clear that he doesn't give a shit and that she can pretty much go fuck herself. Another one burst out laughing to avoid hitting her. That's good, Mireille, not even your mother puts on airs like that. Maybe we're not luminaries but she doesn't seem to care. She has no problem having a good time with us, squealing like a sow the moment your racist father is out there on the road. We take her in twos, sometimes even in threes. What do you think? They crack up, doubling over with laughter, slapping the palms of their hands and high-fiving each other. No surprise that she's friends with that asshole Drissa. He almost lost it because he thought she was totally obsessed with him, when all she really wanted was to have a little fun. At some point in this cacophony of laughter, with all the salacious comments and insults, Mireille took off, horrified and hurt, harboring thoughts about killing somebody. She didn't even look at me, standing there, a silent coward in the shadow of the street lamp. I never ever brought up this delicate subject with her.

Cut it out, guys. It's not cool to talk to someone like that. Show a little respect! Empty words, pretending, when you don't know what else to say, trying to save face, staying close to the guys without overreacting, catching up with Mireille and suffering her anger and disappointment, the fear of subjecting myself to yet another gaze of contempt and disgust. I preferred to take a walk in that moment. I regretted never having accompanied my mother to church, where she goes to pray and recharge her batteries with her sisters in sorrow. I understood this need to be purified, to feel oneself cleansed and unburden the load of each day. To go and find the courage to live joyfully in an intangible world, give yourself to God, and free yourself forever from the nausea, our loyal companion from sunrise to sunset.

I finally understand you, ancestor. You tried and eventually your dreams disappeared with time. All that remains are images and stars from your childhood nights. The socialist lie punctured your youth. Today, Blacks from former allied nations are thrown from trains, and prostitution is commonplace in Cuba. The democratic parody of the Congo has transformed the proud leopards into faithless vultures with an alarming aggression. They are killing each other over a carrion of petrol. Eyes filled with tears no longer know how to cry before the horror they see. Sadly you keep repeating that those improbable black people we used to believe in have all now died. A horrible death. They settled that most cruelly, with a machete and a club, about one million times on the Rwandan hillsides. Black people only ever existed in the sinister holds of slave ships crossing the Atlantic. . . . Ancestor, in the state I'm in today, I understand you much better and I respect your silence.

. . . And to ensure that I don't advance, there are steel bars, and most importantly, an eager captain who's obsessed with me confessing to a murder!

—⚬⚬—

It was around 5:30 PM, Pascal Froment, a civil servant in the national police force in Paris, was preparing to leave his modest home in the inner suburbs to begin the night shift. While he was putting on his jacket, his concerned young wife advised him to be careful. You could hear in her voice that she was nervous. She understood all too well how important Pascal's job was for him. It was just that in light of recent events and the escalating hostility toward police officers, her husband's night shift was making her increasingly anxious. She was trying her best not to annoy him with her worrying, but ever since their little girl was born, the idea of losing him or even just knowing that he might be in danger was making it difficult at times for her to sleep at night. In fact the subject kept coming up and was at the core of many of their discussions, leading to more and more heated arguments.

Pascal had chosen his line of work out of conviction. He had a mission to help the weakest in society, an almost chivalrous vision of law enforcement, one of the few in the police force who believed in what he was doing in the face of the reigning disillusionment among his colleagues. He wanted to present a positive image of his profession, one in which it was possible to have a dialogue and show respect toward both the victims and wrongdoers. He was very much appreciated for his sense of fairness, his honesty, and his kindness. Some, on the other hand, made fun of him and criticized him for always trying to understand, when as far as they could tell, all that was needed was a show of strength and determination. It's us against them. Pascal Froment had developed his own idea about compromise. He was always focused on keeping the peace and tried to act more like a mediator, especially between the different communities. That said, he was well aware of the fact that the police department had the reputation for being deeply racist.

His wife was not concerned with these issues. She just wanted her husband for her and their newborn baby, rather than have him fully devote his time to these ungrateful people who were, moreover, dangerous. She reckoned that their marriage and family life shouldn't come at such great cost, the ridiculously long hours, nights, weekends.... His superiors seemed to have no heart whatsoever. At least his salary should reflect the enormous sacrifices they had to make in their home life.

Only too aware of all this, Pascal Froment did his best to stay cheerful most of the time, took the time to talk with his wife before leaving for work, showing her a lot of attention and love, reassuring her, being funny and affectionate. From the steering wheel of his new car, he would blow kisses as he drove away. He was always making her laugh, playing the drunk driver having a hard time getting out of the driveway and then he would gradually disappear.

It was always the same scene, heavy traffic on the roads going in the other direction from Paris to the suburbs, aggressive drivers, gripped to the wheel, rushing to get back home after an interminably long workday. But for him, it was sheer freedom, the roads were wide open, empty both in front of him and behind him, which made it easy for him to concentrate calmly and prepare for his shift. He drove, relaxed, peacefully, comforted in the fact that he had a loving wife and a job he was passionate about.

He felt a deep and sincere love for his wife. In the last six months, their marriage had been crowned with the birth of their little girl Marie. It was now ten years since he had become a police officer. He still had the same freshness, the same desire to get out onto the streets of Paris, at the wheel of his car, to track down the criminals and resolve violent conflicts. Arbitrating fights among drunkards gave him a real feeling of satisfaction of being in charge of an important mission because it was highly rewarding. It gave him a real sense of purpose. After two years of patrolling, his colleague, a few years younger than him, was already expressing his disillusionment about the profession. All of this doesn't change anything! His frustration and consumption of alcohol were on the rise. It took a lot of effort and some serious threats from Pascal to get him to stop concealing his habit of drinking on their shift.

Once Pascal arrived at the station, he was basically with his second family. First, he went and changed. He had a few polite exchanges in the locker room and caught up on how things had gone down from those coming in from the previous shift. One police officer was especially amazed by Pascal's unwaveringly good mood. He responded with a huge smile. This was exactly what he was proud of. He waited around a little bit. His partner had mastered the art of being systemically late for his shift, but Pascal didn't hold that against him. After a good fifteen minutes, he finally showed up and had to listen to a good dressing down from the police commissioner. Cranky as usual, he said a quick hello to Pascal. Once they were both ready and seated in car number 357, the security controls turned on and the beat assignment in hand, they left the grounds of the police station.

As usual, Pascal, happy to get into action, never failed to find a reason to go on about how great the profession was. His partner kept sinking further into resentment. He was sick of all the Black and Arab pests, all these people that had to come into the world in such great numbers, just so that they could piss off the rest of us, and worst of all everyone hates us, you would think that we were the bad guys in this crazy scenario. They had a relatively calm evening and night, mostly identity checks, conflicts between minors, a routine patrol. About half an hour toward the end of their shift, late in the evening while they were taking a break at a stop sign to get their last wind, a male individual, Black, by all appearances very intoxicated came staggering up to the patrol car and started urinating on the front of the hood. Realizing that his partner was already out of control, Pascal Froment immediately got out of the car to defuse the situation. He knew all too well how situations like these could escalate pretty fast into something truly fatal. He had better take charge of the situation and not waste a second.

—⁂—

You'll soon be going before the judge. Don't even think you can get out of this with your bullshit African nonsense about sorcerers and God knows what. Your parents, your tragic childhood, your neighborhood, and all that crap. We've heard it all before and no one gives a shit! You're getting the maximum. Delinquents like you always wind up caving in and confessing.

Before leaving, the lady officer, even more beautiful than during the interrogation, held a towel out to me. I can finally wash up. She also managed to get me some clean clothes. I need to stay calm. She's smiling. I plan to do exactly as she says. She has my word. I almost burst into tears when she helped me to clean away all that filth in the prison. I had one hand holding up my pants with no belt and the other scrubbing the prison floor, all under the watchful gaze and mockery of the other officers. My fairy came with a floor cloth, a bucket, and a pair of rubber gloves, as a real gesture of humanity.

She then escorts me with two other officers to the shower stalls. All of a sudden I feel like putting an end to this entire comedy by taking myself out. I could grab one of those guns and make the heroic gesture of blowing my skull wide open or just bash my head against the wall until I'm unconscious. But of course I can't even drum up that kind of courage right now. In fact, I feel weary. The nightmare of these past hours has definitely sobered me up. I'm moving so feebly. The proximity to the kind police officer has so completely warmed my heart that I'm finding the strength to keep going. I undress under the vigilant eye of all these officers who are keeping a close eye on me. They are trained to be ready for any and everything. You almost get the feeling that they're just waiting for something to happen so that they can have a go at me again.

The beatings, the blood, and the chains during these last hours have made me forget perhaps, for good, any modicum of modesty. The cold water against my bruised skin is giving me an incredible feeling of happiness. It's as though my very soul is getting cleansed from this washing. It feels like hundreds of invisible hands are moving gently all over my body and my heart spreading pureness and benediction. I'm washing myself now with enthusiasm because I can feel the enormous compassion of the spirits. They're returning from the depths of time to help me through this nightmare. They haven't abandoned me. All is not really lost! Relieved. Showering, I feel somehow exhilarated. It's all coming back to me suddenly. The sequence of events is resurfacing with astounding clarity.

—ᴡᴡ—

The day before yesterday, Mireille left. We were supposed to meet in the Châtelet neighborhood. As usual, I was late. I'd spent the afternoon with Drissa. He's doing a lot better, making a lot more sense, still a long way off, but I'm not giving up hope. He's not smiling yet and definitely not laughing, he needs more time for that, a whole lot of patience and way more work to get there. Suddenly, he started to tell me this strange story about Mireille's mother, as if I don't have enough on my plate already!

He wasn't even fifteen when it had all started. What had been for me a beautiful period in my life had been like a tsunami for him, and I'd been completely unaware of it. He looked me point blank in the eyes with a gaze that said I have nothing more to hide and went on to describe their first afternoon.

As planned, Drissa went by to pick up Mireille, he can't remember where I was at the time. Mireille's mother invited him in and then told him that she was sorry but her daughter would not be home until late that evening, she was out visiting a distant relative of her father's who was suffering from a serious illness. He should have left right then and there. However, blocked, he stood planted in the doorway, trying in vain to find the right words, some form of politesse that would make it easy for him to take off. Only now with the clarity of all his craziness does he recognize the spark that illuminated the look on our friend's mother's face. Whether it was a smell, an idea, or plain old desire, what's clear is that it had not been premeditated. She automatically shut the door behind him and at the same time gently pulled him toward her. She then fixed her eyes, which seemed to really open up for the first time in a very long time, on him. When he went to speak, she tenderly posed her fingers, damaged from all the housework, on his lips. He identified a vague smell of olive oil and cooking that was familiar to him. Gently and with a discreet smile, she guided his hands to her cheeks and without a word led him to her flesh. All while trying to maintain her composure and elegance, she murmured her pleasure, and used her dry fingers to guide the inexperienced fingers of the adolescent at a crazy pace. Her legs trembled and she planted her teeth into his shoulder muscles. She tightened her grip, firmer around Drissa's hands. Drissa, her first folly, beautiful, hot. A few minutes later, the child collapsed, the storm, the pleasure of her body rediscovered, years of sadness forgotten, she reconnected with a level of pleasure that took her to the peak. Then she cried silently and forbid him to ever say a word to anyone.

This was followed by kisses and caresses. She smoothed his hair and complimented him with the crude language only love knows how to make delicious. This fifty-year-old woman was escaping from everything with an adolescent boy at an incredibly delightful pace. She got up and presented her naked body to him, right in his face. She undressed him and guided them to her bedroom. She, who had been taught that love was a simple wave of feelings, far from the body, who had only allowed herself chaste occasional sexual contact with her husband in absolute darkness, dignified controlled breathing, punctuated with the rare I love you, let herself go completely and gave way to infinite carnal delight. She, who never spoke, finally explored the poetry of lips in concert with the tongue, a pulsating novel that flourishes in the depth of the belly and then soars, drowned in love, in silent song, the magic of lovers.

What a sweet symphony for Drissa, a clandestine traveler of tenderness, suddenly all this attention reserved for him. He stayed a while resting on her soft belly, the skin had loosened over time. Tears flowed, not quite knowing what to say to honor the moment.

Drissa didn't want to know how it would end, nor any of the others as a matter of fact. His uncle had seen a patch of black and white hair dancing on his chest while in a trance. He thought that he was going to go on living and being loved for a long time. He takes a drag on his cigarette while squinting his eyes. How long did the relationship last? How come you never told me anything? Drissa smiles from the corner of his eyes, amused. I understand that he just wants me to listen to him. He went to see her several times in their special universe, one in which only a few words were ever exchanged. They took off together toward complete peace and tenderness. She would sigh profoundly, hold him tenderly against her chest, his head in her hands, close her eyes, and smile. A star would glide gently over their skin. They would caress each other, brazenly, loving each other with the fevered hunger of those who had been neglected. In the summertime, their trysts went on amid the racket in the neighborhood. In the fall, they escaped the gloom and cold outside in each other's company. Drissa hopes she did cry from behind the window curtains of her room when the white shirts had come to get him. His final gaze had turned up toward her window.

That was weeks ago now. She has since moved with her husband to a small house about sixty miles or so from Paris, to a well-deserved retirement, far from all the concrete and hate. It's not so much her but more the light and the warmth that Drissa misses.

Three friends enjoying themselves in the parking lot, sometimes, closer to the train station, lulled by the sounds of the RER and cars going full speed at night on the adjacent highway. All smiles, dreams for tomorrow, stoned, hanging in the vacant lot, stealing little wet kisses from Mireille on the nape of my neck, play fighting with Drissa, she would nibble on my tongue and then burst out laughing. And Drissa grumbling where do you think you are? Cut it out, shit, man!

Things definitely cooled down, the initial fascination Mireille and I had for each other after making love when she was having her period. We both contemplated her upper thighs, bathed in red, the blue artery within proximity, the black of her pubis, further below where violet opened up, the pink den and the brown of my private parts resting on her milky white skin. A bouquet of marvelous colors, it was a lovers rainbow!

In a café around Châtelet, Mireille wouldn't stop crying, a real floodgate. I noticed for the first time that she had started to age. Of course she still loves me, that will never change, but she needs another life and for that she has to forget about me and take off far away. Mireille reminded me of my aunts, and some of my mothers' friends. They had this gift for metamorphosing into a huge lamentation, shaking from sobbing, loud hiccups, eyes red, buried in their tissues folded up at least a dozen times. They would lose all sense of modesty, disregard the least ounce of dignity, and were pretty much ready to be consoled by anyone who would open their arms to them, so that they could relay, without interruption and for the umpteenth time the film of the thousand miseries of their little insignificant existences. Mireille, the Amazonian, was wearing the same mask of neglect in the superb way she carried herself, her face swollen from crying.

Going back to Israel, where there is still a war to win, people to save. Did she ever know about Drissa and her mother? Still a mystery. I have myself to think about. I don't even bother to ask the question. She's clearly afraid of falling into the black hole of oblivion that she has always felt so close to her. She sobs a little bit more. I only hear her say that she loves me, finally she is telling me after so many years, it's good to finally hear it. Yet, these three words feel like a huge slap in the face! The death knell of lovers. My legs are starting to tremble, my heart is racing like crazy, a rancid and painful tide floods my whole body. I wish I could cry or even howl out my suffering. I can hear deep down inside an animal screaming in agony.

She loves me and so leaves me to my fate. In truth, I'm suffocating. I'm staying strong. The world is yours for the taking. Even if I'd have preferred to throw myself at her feet, cover them with kisses and implore her, beg her, tuck my dignity away in a pocket, and for the rest of my life if I have to, if only she would accept to stay with me. The pride of the predator keeps me stuck to my seat, submitting to the goodbye. Dry eyes. Heart wounded. Dreams and memories shattered. Looking straight ahead. For a split second, I felt like I could have killed her. If I can't have her, then why should anybody else?

I love you. These three words make me feel like I'm worth something. I still haven't brought up Drissa. I'm hanging on firmly to this declaration that marks the end. My life feels more than ever like a disaster. This is definitely not the time to bring up past moments, those times when we were pleasuring the most intimate parts of our bodies, as seals of our eternal union. . . . How time can make noble gestures seem ridiculous, pathetic, repulsive. Drissa is doing better. Our visit came to an end when he suddenly fell asleep right in the middle of our conversation, a cigarette hanging from his mouth. I had to put the cigarette out myself, then like a brother, I took him in my arms and tucked him into bed.

You're a big part of me, Mireille, but believe me, I understand your decision. I would give anything to have it be mine as well. A voice, a growl from the wild beast whispers I must let her go, her own people are calling her. A beautiful animal roared, his anger calmed. It's time to let go of her hand resting on the table. There is really nothing more to say.

Three little angels, two black boys, one white girl, petty thieves, giggling, running around together for the last time on the vacant lot that runs alongside the main road. They hover a short while by the buildings and the train tracks and then disappear forever. Mireille has made a run for it, upset, her soul torn apart, her heart in pieces. Go on now, and good luck, I'll take care of the bill. It's my turn anyway. No really, don't worry about it. Excited, Mireille is marching to the crazy gallop of her life, always insatiable, heading right to the limit of what's possible, at record speed. She carefully swallowed up anyone who got in her way. They were interesting but merely short layovers to feed her own path. Mireille, a kind of machine, regulated like clockwork to swallow up and digest men, women, and situations without stopping, so great is her hunger and insatiable thirst for wanting more and for things that are different, and these have only increased over time. I was undoubtedly a big piece to swallow, but she finally managed it, and now leaves me here without her, abandoned, cast aside like any old object, of no further interest. Long before me, Drissa had been one of her first victims. Today, she's filled with contempt for him.

One last time, dreaming about her. I see her swaying her large, ample backside she seems to have a hard time carrying. She walks unsure of her footing. Mireille is leaving me. In pain but already in a hurry, she realizes she came tonight to carry out a dirty job, hurtful but necessary, she's finally broken free and is already beginning to exist elsewhere. She's on her way to the Promised Land. She quickly disappears, swallowed up by the metro. This is the perfect word. She's swallowed up, after which there is nothing, total silence, no applause. The first and last spectator is having a hard time leaving the theater. The play really pinned him to his seat. Sitting alone now, in the dark, remembering the most intense scenes. I don't want to think about the outside world and all the problems that await me.

A veil of darkness, each time a little bit thicker, is settling on the streets of Paris, sneaking its way under the Pont au Change. It has already covered over the Pont des Arts. Over there, the Place Saint-Michel, and at the foot of the fountain other hearts are happy to meet up in a languishing tender embrace, warm round breasts pressing against the chest, heart pulsating on the inside. Not a single trace of Mireille or me or of our kisses. It's as though it never happened. A Bakongo, a Jew, a Black guy, a White girl, just another mixed race couple on the streets of Paris. Who cares? Curtain, please.

Later on, I called up Ludovic, who'd also moved to Paris for his studies. He lives in a beautiful furnished studio not far from the Place d'Italie. Don't worry, bro, there are plenty more fish in the sea.... He's trying to be funny. I'm afraid it'll never be the same like it was with Mireille. I can already see myself just going from one girl to the next, from one relationship to another. I always felt that I'd not been mistaken about Mireille, you know that ease you have spending hours with your beloved, that exceptional person. I saw the changes over the last few months more like an episode in an eternal love story. Our love story. Demoralized, I can just see myself heading to the whorehouse with the other guys in the neighborhood, doing precisely what most revolted Mireille.

I meet up with Ludovic at Montparnasse; he's in good spirits and suggests that we head to Rue de Rennes and wander from café to café. It's one of the first days of spring, the most beautiful time of year in Paris. People are coming and going, taking their time, women so happy to finally put on their floral dresses, the plunging necklines hinting ever so slightly at the breasts, with just the right amount showing, some cheerful colored hats, with huge smiles on their faces. Night has just fallen and the café terraces are packed! Ludovic is chatting away, laughing, doing his best to get my mind off things. The streets are full, people bumping into each other but everyone's in good spirits, sorry, go ahead, no problem, a light friendly tap on the shoulder. My head is somewhere else though, somewhere between two and three bodies of water. I'm doing my best to keep my eyes open and to take in some of the good May vibes. But I'm really struggling. The feeling of solitude weighs heavily. Ludovic is like a radio you listen to in the distance, absent-mindedly at the steering wheel on a long journey, he tells me that he's been hanging out all year long, has spent too many nights in nightclubs, smoked up too many joints in the university cafeteria, messed around with loads of girls, shit, man, you've got to make the most of student life!

We're somewhere on a bridge. Some guys come up to us. We share a drink with them. Hilarious and all excited, they tell us that they've just knocked about a bunch of cock-sucking bourgeois students. I'm really not in the mood for this kind of shit. The guy telling us all this is black, with the kind of face that would frighten the CRS police. He's sitting down, elbows on his knees, a joint in one hand and a bottle of rum in the other. He's constantly spitting and he's got some brass knuckles. I know all too well the other side of his gaze. He oozes gratuitous violence, an almost sexual urge to hurt somebody and to get off from it. I can feel Ludovic's panicking. I try to play along. My family and I are so proud I got my high school diploma. I'm almost somebody now with my student ID card, and all that to find myself hiding out at night by the Seine. I'm really getting tired of not resembling what I imagine myself to be. What are you doing? Who are you anyway? You a Rasta or what?

Open all your drawers, change all the labels, or why don't you just burn all of them joyfully once and for all and throw them in the river. Give me a swig, bro. I use the tone I know he can relate to, let me take a puff, cousin, yeah, cool, thanks, hey, hey, we're flying.

Ludovic is back in a good mood again. His carefree spirit has always amazed me. For him, nothing ever seems to really be a problem. He drinks with a bunch of guys who are potentially dangerous. It bothers him in the moment, and then he moves on. He's forgotten. Who are these guys? What are they doing bumming around at night hassling people who are different from them? There you go, at least two more questions for you, my friend. I realize that I have also been somewhat contaminated by the onslaught of questions, precisely what torpedoed Drissa. Ludovic isn't worried. He's just messing around. He visits his parents regularly on their small private estate not far from the old neighborhood, takes holidays overseas, Easter holidays, Christmas in the countryside or at his grandparents, most likely a nice church wedding once he's done with his studies, no more getting stoned and shit-faced, time to focus on his career and get on the saving-up-for-a-down-payment-plan.

We're talking up a storm, drinking a lot; everybody's taking care of himself. Now that she's left me, he admits, helped along by the huge firecracker he's getting baked-out on, he would have gladly tapped that little Mireille, taken her from behind, standing up, or laying down. I'm surprised to see myself laughing along with him.

Ludovic suddenly started talking about some distant cousin who was throwing a party that night, why not head over there and check it out, sounded good to me in the state I was in. I imagined a fierce ambiance, good vibes, some seriously good looking women, nice curves and all, music blasting from the sound system, a nice little hook up for the night, the good life . . . I couldn't care less anyway. Today, I would do whatever with whomever. Fifteen-minute wait for a taxi. I'll never understand Parisian taxi drivers, you're prepared to pay to go someplace, and they have to make a whole science out of it, analyzing you from head to toe, slowing down but never actually stopping. Racial profiling, of course! I shove my wrists into the bottom of my pockets. I'm trying to keep my head up as high as possible so as not to give away my drunken state and my death-warmed-overlook. It's a nice balmy night. I'm not in the mood to rot away here on the sidewalk. A car finally stops. Ludovic's all excited. The driver of the Mercedes is black. I go ahead and start to flatter him, going on about the solidarity among brothers, if only he knew how I was lying. I couldn't give a shit. To hell with all of you! I just need a couple more glasses. Ludovic just wants to blow his load with the first bitch he stumbles across. If I weren't so fucked up, I would make him shut it with a real kick in the mouth. To be honest, I never really could stand the guy. He's one of those people you get so used to over time that you don't even really stop to ask yourself if he's someone you really want to spend time with. Ludovic is basically like a part of the fabric of my life. Like others, he's a part of my journey. He's reassuring. I'm so afraid to be alone!

We get out of the car into the coolness of the night. It's crazy how time flies at night. The street is deserted and I'm having a hard time standing up straight. The urge to dance I was feeling in the car is gone now. I feel like a zombie. One foot before the other, a faint clarity allows me to give short rash answers to my friend's enthusiasm. I advance painfully down the stairs. Each step distills its dose of suffering and demands extraordinary effort. Where does Ludovic get all this energy? Mireille, Mireille, my heart feels like it's about to explode! When we finally enter the apartment where the party is supposed to be taking place, the scene is somewhat pathetic. A blonde girl, her mouth slathered in red wine, moves her body clumsily in the space that's supposed to be a dance floor. If I weren't so heartbroken, maybe I might have found her pretty, but I'm somewhere else. No magic in the world will bring Mireille to me in this very moment. It's laughable even to imagine that she might just suddenly surface out of the blue just because I love her. Two guys slouching on the couch are passing a massive spliff half-heartedly back and forth between them. We're greeted by Ludovic's cousin, who assures us that the party is just getting warmed up, and how cool it is that we stopped by. Something tells me that nobody else is going to be coming. While I'm trying to be friendly with the two potheads, Ludovic is busy trying out some kind of rhythmless dance moves with the wasted blond girl. A few minutes later, they're kissing frantically. The hallucinogenic is making me feel good, I'm smoking, I'm drinking, talking about Mireille and the Kongo sorcerers to my two new sidekicks of the moment. In no time at all, Ludovic and the blonde chick are completely wrapped up in each other, tongues hanging out and everything. In my drunken state, it's difficult for me to keep up with their erotic moves. They've barely made it into the room next door and you can hear them grunting like animals, the wood of the parquet creaks as if someone had just smashed themselves against it. The blonde girl sounds like she's caught in some kind of hysterical laughter. They didn't even bother to close the door.

The two guys, practically falling asleep by now, are having a good laugh as well. They keep taking turns at some pretty salacious commentary. One of them regrets being so fucked-up, cos he might have been able to take a hit as well without this drunken bitch ever having a clue.

I can feel I've had enough. I want to go home now, see Mireille and Drissa again, and talk to some of the benevolent spirits. So, I go on a rant insulting my fellow smoking buddies for their vulgarity, you're complete morons, but these guys are elsewhere, ignore me, bad trip, they mutter to each other, giggling. My need for the warmth of a home has made me nasty. Suddenly my stomach starts acting up and bubbling. Thick, disgusting bile fills my mouth. I try to get up but I'm staggering, my body abandons me and I vomit in convulsive pain all over the poor guys, offended of course. Between hiccups, I insult them with a vengeance, throwing my fist out every which way while heading for the exit. On my way out, I bump into Ludovic in his boxers, alerted by the commotion. He rushes out of his love nest, let him go to hell, I've never been able to stand him, I escape into the solitude of the night.

I eventually find myself down by the quays. I decide to go and have one last drink over by the Place Sainte-Opportune. I stagger over to Les Halles, head down, and finally settle into a seat at the bar, La Cervoise. Pedro, the Peruvian barman, who I know very well, serves me an outstanding beer. He's talking to me without even noticing that both ears and brain have pretty much shut down for the night.

As usual, he beats me at a game of craps, which gives him quite the thrill and then he starts to put up the tables and chairs for the night. The guy has the gift of gab. I can no longer fight off the fatigue. My head is heavy. I'm only able to hold it up by sticking my mouth to the beer glass. I'm drooling on the side, pathetic. I'm disgusted with myself! Too bad for the girl who thought I was cute. Pedro quiets down. The evening is winding down. I have no desire for anything!

I've really had too much to drink and smoke. La Cervoise closed up, so I started to just wander aimlessly on the deserted streets. I think that I first fell backward and tried painstakingly to get up by leaning onto the front of the dark blue station wagon, number 357 of the national police force. Back on my feet, I opened my zipper and started to relieve myself. The urge was too pressing. Urinating gave me an intense satisfaction that I felt in my whole body.

Police. What's going on with you? Take it easy. You don't have to carry on like this because you can't hold your drink. Come on, that's enough! He stood before me with this saddened look, compassionate, holding his hands out to help me up. My neurons are short-circuiting and I think I showed him quite blatantly a contemptuous smile. His partner, outraged and disgusted, was sounding off, fucking shit, for fuck's sake, I can't believe assholes like this exist! He claims that I roared with laughter, head falling back like a lunatic, opening my arms in the shape of a cross. He couldn't do anything. It all happened so fast. Pascal was too idealistic, he wasn't careful enough. Today the streets are filled with all kinds of unknown riffraff. You can't just walk down the street, relaxed, imagining it belongs to you. I hit him, pushed him, bit him, gave him some pretty hefty kicks in the head even though he was already down and lifeless. Thudding sounds against a skull on the asphalt. Let him take his load too, take his share of the suffering. At first he pleaded and then he finally shut up for good. There was blood everywhere. He must have thought about his wife, his daughter, and maybe he even recalled the young guy, crying on his brother's shoulder, one day, not far from the Eiffel

Tower. Afterward, there were handcuffs, screams, more beatings, a real maelstrom of violence all around me. I'm falling asleep standing up, appeased, relieved.

Now I'm a criminal, captain, you can go home now, but you had better make sure that you have locked the door and put on the dead-bolts. Yes, gentlemen of the court, I pissed out all my frustrations, on the officer, my fear of the future, the love that left me, a devastated Congo, my friends' distress, petrol the color of blood, the cement in my veins, rage in my eyes, and the invisible ones I no longer hear. Keep your ears open, let your eardrums quiver before my outcry and answer the call. It's the urine of the wild cat that we alone can distill. I pissed on the officer and I beat on him pretty badly. To all these ridiculous questions that keep tormenting my life, I answered with calm fits of rage. What are you anyway, French or African? I hit where it hurt most and with everything I had, again and again! Once the evening, the sirens, the police cars flashing blue lights, the words behind the voices, the swarm of indecipherable images, when all of it had finally come to an end, I stood there standing. I didn't even smile or cry. All I wanted was to sleep.

Drissa has been quiet for a longtime now, like the silence at home. Emptiness surrounds me. In the hospital where I came into this world, rats and dogs are mercilessly fighting over the cockroaches in the corridors. You basically enter the hospital to die on the bare mattresses, with no sheets. No one even thinks about repainting the walls.

A bunch of lost kids meticulously strip the dying of whatever they have left. Over there in my father's village, the mobongui fire no longer illuminates more than half a dozen abandoned old men, with sad expressions and jaundiced, glassy eyes. Idle spirits dance and wait calmly, inaccessible, hidden in the darkness. During the past several years, the Chinese have returned home to build Capitalism in the Empire, still Communists in the Underworld. Carole is taking care of her pregnancy and will be a new mother in four months. She's waiting patiently for Drissa to fully regain his faculty. She wants to start a family with him. The ancestor has done his time. On the bank, next to the Congo River where in the past you were meant to drown yourself, militiamen have built a torture chamber and an arbitrary detention space. Mireille has disappeared; tears in her eyes saying never ever again, forget even my name. We have lost trace of pious Kamel somewhere in a military training camp in Yemen. The guys from the neighborhood are preparing for a football match in the parking lot. As for me, I've savagely assassinated an officer of the law; an executive of legitimate violence, a responsible, loving, family man.

Make sure to lock the metal bars behind me, wall me up, set up the watch tower, fill it with trigger-happy snipers, release your watch dogs, you will never be able to rip out the heart of a wildcat. I wear the marks of the leopard in my loins. Captain, keep your airtight uniform on, firmly lace up your shiny black boots from the ankle up to the neck, pay attention to the openings, adjust your baseball cap and make sure it's pointed before your eyes before I lick you! I have the instinct of the bush. I'm thriving, endlessly regenerating. I have the heart of the jungle. Hidden within me is a force you could never imagine, a furnace with inexhaustible resources. With its support, I have regained my bearings, thanks to the wisdom of my forefathers. This is and remains my most loyal companion.

—⁓—

I don't want to have to hear any more of your questions, I'm done. You can always ask them but they'll never affect me. They'll just glide and ricochet off my head. Look, they're all smashing horribly to the floor, as trivial as spit, ugly, insignificant. They dry up and disappear, in no time at all. Your questions, I'm propelling them, going forward, far from me. I'm sending them flying where they will never find me. If, for whatever reason they come back to bother me, even for the shadow of a split second, like pollen in the nose at springtime, I will effortlessly sneeze them all out right back at you!

Captain, I'm like Drissa, I've left. You only have my body, this car-cass of doubts and complexes on which to unleash your fears, your hate, your civil penal code, whatever you want, but as for me, I'm out of here, ciao! You'll never be able to catch up with me, seize me. I'm too clever for that. Good riddance, from here on out, I'm going to be very careful, especially with my head.

Given that Drissa and I look like no one else, we will remain standing! Together, we will continue to pull each other along, always higher, more agile, marvelous, strange, extraordinary. I'll take his hand so that we can perfect our great leaps, the ones that we'll weave among continents, worlds, and times. This is the real masterpiece of tomorrow.

We will swallow up the distances; powerless they will collapse on our path! Starting today, we will resist questions, weapons, and medication. You will not have my skin, captain, not you, not the judges, not Mireille, no one! You won't ever have Drissa's either, for I know he's watching out and I'm minding out for him!

Wilfried N'Sondé was born in 1969 in the Congo (Brazzaville) and grew up in France. He is widely considered one of the shining lights of the new generation of African and Afropean writers. His work has received considerable critical attention and been recognized with prestigious literary awards, most notably the Prix des Cinq Continents de la Francophonie and the Prix Senghor de la création littéraire.

Karen Lindo is a scholar of French and Francophone Literatures who taught in the United States for several years and is currently teaching and translating in Paris.

Dominic Thomas has published numerous books and edited volumes on the cultural, political, and social relations between Africa and France, and on immigration and race in Europe, including *Black France* (Indiana University Press, 2007) and *Africa and France* (Indiana University Press, 2013), and has translated works by Aimé Césaire, Faïza Guène, Alain Mabanckou, and Abdourahman Waberi. He is the Global African Voices series editor at Indiana University Press.

CPSIA information can be obtained at www.ICGtesting.com
Printed in the USA
BVOW08s1055120716

455252BV00002B/34/P